CHANGE YOUR THOUGHTS CHANGE YOUR FEELINGS

Plus other short stories and snippets

Mary Lewsley

Grosvenor House
Publishing Limited

The right of Mary Lewsley to be identified as the author of this
work has been asserted in accordance with Section 78
of the Copyright, Designs and Patents Act 1988

The book cover is copyright to Mary Lewsley

This book is published by
Grosvenor House Publishing Ltd
Link House
140 The Broadway, Tolworth, Surrey, KT6 7HT.
www.grosvenorhousepublishing.co.uk

This book is a work of fiction. Any resemblance to
people or events, past or present, is purely coincidental.

A CIP record for this book
is available from the British Library

ISBN 978-1-83615-138-8

About the Author

Mary Lewsley is the pen name of Maureen McMullan. She was born in Birmingham to Irish parents. Mary Lewsley was her mother's birth name.

Mary's father (Maureen's grandfather) died when Mary was just a babe in arms. So in honour and recognition of her mother and the grandfather she never knew, Maureen wanted her pen name to be Mary Lewsley.

Maureen is passionate about Ireland and in 1997, together with her partner, bought a small Irish farmhouse in the hills of Kerry overlooking the beautiful little town of Kenmare. She feels so delighted and proud to have put life back into a little pocket of the country she loves so much.

She spends her time between England and her second home in Ireland, which has influenced many of her stories. Her first book of short stories, Wee Row of Shops and a Bar, was partly inspired by the delightful little town of Kenmare.

Acknowledgements

Thank you to my daughter, Michelle Meli, for taking the time out of her busy work schedule to proof read and profile edit my stories.

Thank you to my son, Adam Meli, for his continual support and encouragement and lifting my spirits, when I doubted myself.

Thank you to my beautiful grandchildren, Jay and Lauren Hextall, for the cover photo. Lauren for modelling so beautifully and Jay for pressing the camera shutter at precisely the right time. Although Lauren would say that she directed the pressing of the trigger. I call it one superb joint effort.

Thank you to my friend Marian Beddows for reading my stories, before publication, and giving me her honest feedback.

Thank you to my partner Alan Freeman for all the support, meals, sandwiches and cups of tea. Not to mention help with my outdated laptop.

Finally, thank you to Grosvenor House Publishing Limited for making it happen.

Synopsis

Change Your Thoughts Change Your Feelings is a collection of short stories and what Mary calls snippets: very short works, mainly of observation.

It is an ideal book to take travelling when one doesn't have the space to carry the luxury of more than one book. This collection of short stories is extremely varied and holds the reader's attention. Some of the stories have little twists, bringing unexpected and surprising endings.

These are stand alone stories, unlike Mary's first book, Wee Row of Shops and a Bar, in which the first eight stories were linked through the friendship and life experiences of the characters.

Contents

1

Change Your Thoughts
Change Your Feelings

Jane Lucas awoke startled by the sound of the doorbell. The progress of the sunrise was an indication that she had overslept.

"Oh shit, shit" could be heard as she tried to navigate her way into the inside out sleeves of her dressing gown. *Thank God for the postman*, she thought.

Jane worked at her local Health Centre in suburban Nottingham. She had the responsibility of opening up today. It was also Wednesday; the day she held her weekly anxiety support group.

I better wear my red pants today, I think I need grounding. Unbalanced chakras are not the way to start the day.

A quick brush and floss, a wet flannel in the appropriate places, followed by a quick squirt of deodorant and she was out of the door.

Despite Jane having a hectic start to her day, morning surgery was surprisingly quiet. No irate patients, screaming children, or nonstop telephone calls. The perfect recipe to make a relaxing transition from practice nurse to anxiety support group facilitator.

Jane was in no doubt that talking about their anxieties and fears was a great comfort and support for sufferers. She was in no doubt because she had been there herself. However, she was feeling a little disheartened, when she was observing that some in the group were returning each week with the same script as the week before, picking the same scab that didn't heal. Reaffirming anxiety was still their master. The mind, that powerful tool we cannot touch or see, yet the brain believes every thought it churns out.

When Jane was a child she saw days of the week in colour. She had a different colour for each day of the week. In the magical, imaginative mind of a child that was all pretty normal. Life was pretty normal for Jane, until at the age of 25 she suffered her first panic attack. She tried to carry on with life, but the attacks became more frequent and anxiety was a daily occurrence. It was so debilitating that it forced her to take long-term sick leave. She woke each morning with adrenaline surging into her stomach and ascending into her chest. Her heartbeat pounding, echoing in her ears. There was no respite, each day her anxious thoughts occupied her mind, filling her body with unpleasant and frightening physical sensations.

"Come on Jane, come on. What has happened to you?" she screamed out in frustration.

She had lost herself and somewhere inside she had lost the young Jane who saw days in colours. Now her days were grey and heavy, pressing down on her with impending doom.

As she sat with her anxious thoughts, she realised it was Friday. Fridays used to be green, the colour of nature, nurturing, nourishing, calming, giving her a sense of security. The longer she sat, the more she focused on this beautiful colour until it had encapsulated her very aura, bringing with it all the wonderful feelings that this colour once held for her. She became aware that as she was changing her thoughts, she was changing her feelings. It wasn't instant, or long lasting, but it was a start and eventually her road to recovery. Of course some days proved difficult, but she accepted that and told herself, tomorrow would be a better day. All her tomorrows became better days. She had once again become custodian of her mind and master of her thoughts.

Her meeting was about to start. Jane had all the qualifications to understand exactly how they were feeling. She knew it was an arduous task, for some of them, just to attend. Even opening their front door to face the daylight could shock their senses into a panic attack. She watched them file into the room, bringing with them their racing hearts, jelly legs, pounding headaches and other physical weird sensations. So weird they cannot be described.

Jane never shared her anxiety and panic attack experiences: it was their group. However, she did want to share her days in colour. At the risk of being perceived as weird, Jane decided she would add a new dimension to the group. After all it was Wednesday. Wednesdays were red days for Jane, warm, comforting and giving her confidence. *What better day of the week to introduce my colours?* she thought.

Jane always ended the class with a ten minute guided meditation. She thought it would be a wonderful opportunity to incorporate the colours in there. After the calming breathing techniques, the group was given the chance to discuss and share any experiences, good or bad, that had occurred during the week. Of course sitting quietly and just listening was also an option.

The energy in the group seemed particularly flat this week. This confirmed to Jane it was a good week to add a new tool to their anxiety tool box.

Jane took a deep breath and a sip of water before addressing the group, after their comfort break.

"Right everyone, you don't sound as if you have had a good week. So this week I want to share something that is personal to me. Something that I experience and use when I might be having an overwhelming or difficult day." She thought it best not to expand on her own anxiety breakdown. "I also hope, very much, that it might help you."

The energy lifted, she had their attention.

"In our meditation I want you to focus on today, Wednesday. Then ask yourself what colour you think Wednesdays are. What does your colour mean to you? How does it make you feel in a positive way? Surround yourself with your colour until it envelopes your whole body. Feel the feeling, the meaning that comes into your mind."

Jane left them in silent meditation for ten minutes. She signified the end of the session with the mellow sound of her little singing bowl.

"I want you to continue focusing on your colour and your feelings for the rest of the day. Take them home with you. I also have some homework for you. You didn't expect to get homework did you?" Jane laughed.

"I want you to do the same meditation each day. Write down your colours together with your feelings and the meanings that come with it. Do your meditations in the mornings, then place yourself in a bubble of your colour for the rest of the day and let your body feel the positive feelings that it signifies."

One member of the group asked, what the purpose of meditation was.

"That is a good question Dianne. The aim of this meditation is to change your thoughts. If you master the art of changing your thoughts, you automatically change your feelings. If you have a wobble during the week, don't resist it, accept it, go with the flow and breathe. At the same time focus on your wonderful bubble of colour, your protection from that pesky little gremlin that tries to invade your mind."

Jane observed a little excitement in the air as the group left the meeting. Almost like little children leaving Santa's grotto, clutching their present. They were clutching hope: the totally invisible present.

In the weeks that followed, Jane was overjoyed as the dynamics in the group were changing. Most of the group had ripped up their usual scripts and replaced them with shared days of colour and positive feelings. There were days when that pesky anxiety gremlin came knocking. The more time passed, the more difficult it was for him to break through that protective bubble of colour.

Who would have thought that my childhood days of colour would make such a big impact for others and indeed myself, she thought.

The meetings definitely seemed lighter and to add a little more lightness to the group, Jane would ask in pantomime style,

"What do we do when we change our thoughts?"

The group would respond, "Change our feelings."

It amused everyone. For Jane to see their smiles and hear their laughter, was well worth the risk of being perceived as weird, back on that red Wednesday afternoon.

2

The Riddle

The offices of Simpkins and Geoffries Solicitors were a little drab to say the least. The walls were dressed with the darkest of green wallpaper, accessorised with treacle brown varnished doors and picture rails. Half a dozen or so people chatted away, creating a sombre vibration around the walls. They had gathered together to hear the last will and testament of George Arthur Roberts.

In the 1950s George became a successful self-made business man, creating a small chain of ironmongers that were strategically placed around the West Riding of Yorkshire. His shops were well stocked. They always had that one thing you needed, that you couldn't get anywhere else. If they didn't have it, George prided himself that it would be in stock before the week was out.

Despite his success George's personal life had been rather sad. After fifteen years of a blissful marriage to his dear wife Hilda, she passed away after a short illness. The devoted couple had longed for a family, but sadly it never happened.

George's dilemma before he died was, to whom he should leave the bulk of his estate. George had two brothers, Sydney and Albert. Sydney had one son, Brian. Albert had two sons, Anthony and Graham. George had been very fond of all three of his nephews. They almost felt like his own children.

The heavy varnished door of the solicitor's office was pushed open and the small delicate frame of Henry Simpkins followed through, not looking for one second that he had the strength or energy to open it.

"Ahem. Good morning everyone."

A mumbled "good morning" was reciprocated. Mr. Simpkins was very detailed in his explanation as to why they were there, and very precise and particular when mentioning the names and addresses of beneficiaries.

George's will was very straightforward and to a point uncomplicated. His house and all his monies in bank accounts were to be divided equally between his two brothers, Sydney and Albert, and his three nephews, Brian, Anthony and Graham. George didn't want the ownership of his business to be divided. He wanted it to go to one of his nephews. That way there wouldn't be any arguments about how it would be run. It would stay in the family and hopefully be passed down to future generations. George was a kind man and didn't want to choose a nephew, in case it displayed favouritism, which could lead to family rivalry.

After the will was read Mr. Simpkins then went on to say,

"I now have a letter to read that is addressed to Brian, Anthony and Graham."

The three young men glanced at each other, all of them looking very bemused, although it did cross their minds that the business would be divided between them.

Mr. Simpkins cleared his throat and took a sip of water.

Dear Brian, Anthony and Graham,

I hope this letter finds you all well. As you know, you have been in my life since the day you were born. I have loved all three of you without exception. I regarded you like the children I never had. I do not wish the content of this letter to cause any disagreement between you. I ask you to respect my wishes and please play along with them."

"Play along with them?" Brian whispered under his breath.

"I am going to leave my business to one of you, but I can't choose which one. Therefore, I have

written a riddle and whoever can solve the riddle will find the key to my safe, where you will find the deeds to my shops and become the new owner of G. Roberts Ironmongers. The key is hidden somewhere on my property, either inside, outside, on top of, or underneath. In other words, it could be anywhere.

The riddle is as follows:

I am warm, cosy and protective to the key, as it lies within, with the birds. I have heard many stories throughout the passage of time. I look cold on the outside, but am very warm on the inside. I have been a comfort to many, yet an irritation to some. Where am I?

Good luck boys. I wish whoever finds the key all the luck in the world and continued success with the business. To my two remaining nephews please understand my reasons for leaving the shops to just one of you. Believe me, I have seen too many businesses fail because of disagreements on how to manage. Remember, in life, what is meant to be, will be.

I wish you all happy and successful lives and may God bless you all.

Uncle George.

The nephews were quite overcome, all of them reliving childhood memories with Uncle George and each one of them giving the other a brotherly pat on the back.

As they left the offices of Simpkins and Geofferies, Henry Simpkins handed all three of them a sealed envelope, each containing a copy of the riddle. Brian, Anthony and Graham stood outside the solicitor's office looking even more bewildered than ever.

"Phew. What do reckon of that then?" Brian remarked.

"Well, don't know about you, but I could do with a pint," said Anthony.

Graham agreed that was the best thing anyone had said all day.

Pints were ordered. Glasses were raised.

"Uncle George." toasted Brian. Echoed with "Uncle George." "Uncle George."

"By heck that were a turn up. Who'd 'ave thought we'd 'ave riddle to solve." Graham said

"Aye and I 'aven't a clue what he's talking about." Anthony laughed.

"Well we've plenty of food for thought, that's for sure," exclaimed Brian. "Who's for another one?"

All three young men went to bed with the same puzzling thoughts going round and round in their heads: The Riddle.

Brian thought he'd cracked it.

George loved his pigeons and the riddle said the key lay with the birds. Uncle George did talk to his pigeons; that could be the stories. The pigeon loft was warm on the inside and could be cold on the outside. They were a comfort to George, but Hilda hated them. That's got to be it, its got to be. What else could it be? he thought.

He felt very excited. He reminisced about the times he spent with Uncle George and his pigeons. He could see him with his flat cap and pipe between his teeth. He could almost hear George saying,

"I'll hold 'im lad and you can stroke his neck. Gently does it. By 'eck, I reckon he likes you, he's cooing away."

Brian smiled. "Night night Uncle George, rest in peace."

Brian loved Uncle George and he loved his pigeons. Tomorrow he was going to take that pigeon loft apart.

Anthony also lay awake trying to solve the riddle. He did have thoughts about part of the riddle, but couldn't quite piece it all together. Anthony thought the birds could be three flying ducks that Aunt Hilda had hung above the fireplace many years ago. There was a hook underneath where Uncle George hung his cap to keep it warm.

He could have hung the key under his cap. It would be warm, cosy and protected by his cap. And underneath the birds. Anthony thought.

He couldn't quite work out a comfort to some and an irritation to others.

Oh well. I'll just have to sleep on it. I'll go over there in t'morning to take a look.

Graham on the other hand hadn't got the slightest inkling about the riddle and he didn't expect Brian or Anthony would either. He was far too tired to concentrate on solving riddles. Common sense Graham thought it much better to get his head down and wake up refreshed.

Morning had broken and Graham's sub-conscience mind must have been whirring away while he slept. His first thought was of a teapot Aunt Hilda used to use. He remembered it so well; it was cream porcelain, with three pretty birds of blue and green sitting on a branch that circled around the pot. Graham's thoughts were calm and considered.

Maybe they are the birds in the riddle. The key could be in the teapot. The stories would be people chatting away over a cup of a tea. The teapot would be warm on the inside when full of tea, but it wouldn't be cold on the outside. I can see how it would be a comfort, but not an irritant.

It was amazing that not twenty-four hours had passed since Brian, Anthony and Graham had been presented with Uncle George's riddle and they had all come up with a potential solution.

The three young men all made their way to George's house, none of them knowing the others were going. When Anthony arrived Brian was already there. Graham arrived last. Yesterday in the pub, they had set some ground rules. They all agreed that if one of them had started searching in a particular area, then neither of the other two would search in the same place.

Brian was at the pigeon loft searching every nook and cranny inside and out.

Anthony was in the parlour. He didn't have much searching to do. Uncle George's cap was hung on the hook beneath the three flying ducks. He felt his heart beating as he moved towards the fireplace. Lifting his hand slowly he gently took George's cap off the hook. There was no key.

Graham had gone straight to the kitchen. Aunt Hilda's teapot was on the Welsh dresser. Graham was calm, he remembered what Uncle George had said, "what will be, will be." The lid rattled as Graham lifted the teapot down. Something slid about inside. "Oh my Lord," said Graham. The ever calm and tranquil Graham had a little surge of adrenaline. He gingerly removed the lid and there inside was a bundle of safety pins.

"Ee by gum. Now I'm scuppered."

He walked into the small reception room they called the snug. He wanted to sit in a comfy armchair and have a think. He had memories of Uncle George in that room, even the cushion that he used to fall asleep on, as he sat on George's lap, was still there. It used to be a beautiful pale blue, but with the passage of time it had become a little grubby. Despite Graham's brusk voice, he was quite sentimental at heart. He picked up the cushion and held it close to his chest.

Brian had almost dismantled the pigeon loft when he was joined by Anthony.

"It's ok Brian I am only coming to see how thee are, I ain't interferin'."

"Oh that's ok Ant, there's nowt here. Did you have any luck?"

"Nowt at all. Let's go and look for our Graham. He was rummaging round t'kitchen when I left."

The house was quiet. The kitchen was empty. The parlour door was closed just as Anthony had left it. The door to the snug was slightly ajar. As they pushed it open they were confronted with Graham covered in feathers. He looked quite ashen. Brian leant over him.

"You ok Lad? You look like you've seen a ghost."

"I've solved riddle. I've found the key. It was in this cushion, a feather cushion. The birds are the feathers that are warm and cosy, protecting the key. The cushion has heard many stories that Uncle George told me when I sat on his knee. It looks cold on the outside because of the pale blue colour; it's warm on the inside because of the feathers. I always found the cushion very comfortable, but if ever Uncle George had it at his back, he would throw it on t'floor and said it irritated him."

"Blimey Graham how did you work all that out?" said Brian.

"I picked up the cushion, a feather fell out and it all came together."

"Well one thing's for sure," remarked Anthony. "You'll not have to change name over door. It will still be G. Roberts Ironmongers."

3

The Rose Garden

The telephone rang at 8.30am precisely. Lucy Gallagher descended the stairs in a state of half slumber. The sun entered the hallway through the jewelled stained glass windows of the front door, casting colours of red and green onto the black and white floor tiles.

"Hello"

"Hello Lucy?"

"Yes. Who's calling?"

"Lucy, it's Maggie."

"Maggie?"

"Yes Maggie. John's wife, your cousin John. I'm so sorry Lucy, but your mum died yesterday. I'm sorry to tell you such sad news, but we thought you would want to know."

"Oh right. Yes, er, thanks for letting me know. Bye."

Lucy was feeling shocked rather than sad. She had been estranged from her mother, Grace Gallagher, for nearly eight years now. In fact she was estranged from most of her family.

Grace's marriage had been disastrous. She would have welcomed an instruction manual on how to deal with the pitfalls of marriage, with a table of contents ranging from mortgage arrears and debts, other women, a lazy husband and last but not least, the big one, mental and physical cruelty.

Grace's true nature was quiet and reserved. She was gentle and caring, but that had all been taken away. It was lost. Lost, buried deep beneath the rubble of anxiety and fear. Her stress showed to everyone around her, including Lucy. Grace thought Lucy would understand, as she witnessed her mother's physical abuse. Hindsight, as they say, is a wonderful thing, and it certainly was for Grace.

Not a day passed without her thinking about her daughter. She worried about her and hoped she was taking care of herself. Not having her in her life was heartbreaking for Grace. Lucy was soon to be celebrating her 40th birthday. A month previously Grace had decided that she would write to Lucy. She felt a need to convey to her daughter that she was always in her thoughts and missed her terribly.

Lucy walked into the kitchen and flicked the switch on the kettle. Her morning coffee was her salvation. Robotically producing her coffee making ingredients, together with her favourite white mug, she was trying to process the news of her mother's death. She didn't know how to be, how to think, how to feel. Trying to bring her mother's face to mind was not easy, if not impossible. Lucy was unaware she had made her coffee. It was only when she tapped her spoon three times on the side of her mug, did she realise her morning pick-me-up was ready.

"Oh my God," she said out loud. "She used to do that." She being her mother Grace Gallagher.

When Maggie had told Lucy her mother had died yesterday, yesterday was Friday, two days before Lucy's birthday on Sunday. Walking into the conservatory Lucy flopped into her chair. The silence of the room was interrupted by gentle raindrops tapping away on the glass ceiling.

Is my life beginning at 40, or am I having a mid-life crisis? were the thoughts running through Lucy's mind. She was beginning to feel that the news of her mother's death was just a bloody inconvenience, an inconvenience to her thoughts, to her emotions. She really wanted to keep it at the back of her mind and let it stay there. Lucy didn't have any siblings, but her mother had two and enough nephews and nieces to deal with funeral arrangements.

She sipped her coffee, then said, "Ah that's good."

Oh no, she thought. She always used to say that. Always after her tea, she would say, Ah that's good.

Again 'she' and 'her' were referring to her mum. The woman who 40 years ago tomorrow, gave her life. Life with all the expectations of happiness.

Grace often said to Lucy, "Don't expect anything in life, then you won't be disappointed."

Of course Grace was verbalising her own feelings wrapped up in advice for Lucy. She never opened up her heart to anyone; she didn't think she was worthy enough for anyone to listen.

As tomorrow was Sunday some of her friends were taking her to David Austen's rose gardens, one of her favourite places to be. Lucy's friends were allowing her to choose four roses, one for each decade of her life. It was to be their birthday gift to her.

As she sat in thought, Lucy heard the letterbox slam. She rose from her cane chair to pick up the post. Half a dozen or so birthday cards with various coloured envelopes lay on the hall floor, a few of them from old school friends. Scanning the envelopes, she surprised herself by feeling a tinge of sadness that her mother's handwriting didn't appear on any of them. She placed them next to the phone on the hall table and promised herself she wouldn't open them until tomorrow. As for today, she was going to go into town to treat herself to a new outfit for her visit to the rose gardens and to simply say "Happy 40th birthday to me."

As Lucy went to bed that night, she was determined to enjoy her day tomorrow and was adamant she wouldn't be sharing the news of her mother's death. It's not as if she talked about her anyway.

Lucy and her friends Ann, Jackie and Dawn were arriving at the rose gardens. Jackie had no interest in gardening and couldn't understand Lucy's excitement. Her excitement grew when she was told she could choose four roses as her birthday gift. Although inside her heart her feelings were shadowed by sadness. She kept thinking that 40 years ago today her mother was very much alive and looking forward to the future. Now today she was gone, gone forever.

"Penny for your thoughts Lucy. Are you deciding which colour to buy?" Jackie said.

If only she knew my thoughts, Lucy pondered fleetingly.

"Yes, do you have any colours in mind?" Ann enquired.

"Well I have prepared a bed for a couple, but now I have your generous gift, I know where I could put two containers. I was thinking of oranges, apricots and maybe yellows. They would all complement each other."

"Sounds beautiful." Dawn agreed.

Lucy pointed to the most beautiful apricot rose. "Wow, that's a beauty."

She went closer to read the name on the label. She stood motionless as she read the name was Grace. For the first time since she heard the news of her mother's death, tears filled her eyes. The realisation had set in. She quickly blinked several times to clear them away.

Out of character, Jackie started to take an interest.

"How about this one Lucy? It would complement your rose beautifully. It's a lovely orangey yellow."

"Oh well done Jackie." Lucy laughed. "We'll make a gardener out of you yet."

As she watched her friends walking amongst the roses and making her day special, it made her realise the value of their friendship. It also reminded her that her mother always used to say to her, "Don't wait until tomorrow to appreciate today."

"By the way Jackie, what's the name of the orangey-yellow rose." Lucy called out.

"Oh hang on. It's called, 'Bring Me Sunshine'."

Lucy nearly fell over. 'Bring Me Sunshine' was a song her mother used to sing. Sometimes when she was washing up and always when she was happy. Her mother's voice singing that song was spinning round and round in her head.

"Are you ok Lucy?" Jackie remarked.

"What? Oh I'm fine. Just a bit dizzy. I think it must be the excitement of the day."

"Have you seen these beautiful pink ones over here," Ann shouted out.

"And these white ones." Dawn said.

"No, as beautiful as they are, I have decided to have two of the Grace and two of the Bring Me Sunshine. I don't want too much variation. Less is more. I know they will look stunning."

"Does that mean we can go for a coffee?" said Jackie the ever unenthusiastic gardener.

Lucy was oblivious to Jackie's request. Her thoughts were all consuming. This time last week her life was 'normal'. Her mum was alive, but she didn't think about her, she didn't miss her.

Just one week later, her mum had died and she was choosing roses in remembrance of her. Although strictly speaking the roses chose Lucy. It was almost like Grace had played a part in it. The oddest thing of all to Lucy, was that she was starting to miss her mum.

With all the memories and reminders of Grace over the weekend, from   tapping her spoon three times on her coffee mug and saying "Ah that's good" when she drank it, to finding roses called Grace and Bring Me Sunshine, made Lucy feel she had celebrated her big 40th with her mum. Her cocktail of emotions had the ingredients of sadness, happiness, confusion and regret.

At 11pm after a long, yet happy and lovely day, Lucy's friends delivered her and her beautiful roses safely back home. As she hugged them all tightly she thanked them for a wonderful day.

"I am so lucky to have you and I am so grateful you are my friends. I hope you realise how much I value your friendship."

"Oh don't start getting soppy; you know I can't abide tears." Jackie said in a very hard voice, that was coming from a very soft spot within.

The four friends fell about laughing and had one final hug at the end of their perfect day.

The security light came on in the porch as Lucy put her key in the lock. The brightness of the light startled her, as she woke her body was sweating, her tears flowed uncontrollably into her pillow. As she opened her eyes, her tears together with the early morning sunlight made it impossible for her to focus on the picture in front of her on the bedroom wall. She swiftly ran downstairs to check on the David Austin website to see if there were roses called Grace and Bring Me Sunshine.

"Yes," she screamed, "my roses are real."

She ran downstairs, her roses had gone. There were no cards on the hall table or the mantelpiece. Her dream was so vivid, so real, she wasn't sure what day it was, until the letterbox slammed. As in her dream various coloured envelopes lay on the floor. She quickly scooped them up, her eyes darting over the handwriting. There it was, her mum's handwriting clear and distinct. She hugged it close to her. The phone rang. Her heart thumped hard in her chest. The vividness of her dream made her feel scared. Scared that she would hear the dreaded news of her mum's death. She nervously picked up the phone.

"Hello"

"Hello Lucy?"

"Yes. Who's calling?"

"Lucy it's mum. Happy Birthday. Are you ok?" Grace spoke with a lump in her throat.

Lucy was so overjoyed to hear her mum's voice.

"Thank you Mum. I am so glad to hear you."

"I was going to include a letter in with your card, but I decided against that as I thought It would be much nicer to speak to you. After all, tomorrow was a big day for both of us 40 years ago. I couldn't let it go by without speaking to you. I would like to buy you something special if you would let me."

"Mum, I would love nothing more and I know what you can buy me. I saw them in a dream, but they are very real, as I checked them out on the website. Would you come to the rose gardens with me?"

4

The Rosary Beads

Agnes Scully felt her time on earth was coming to an end. She had planned her funeral, chosen her hymns and had one important wish on her wish list. It was that her rosary beads be placed with her in her coffin, but not any set of beads. They had to be the special mother of pearl rosary beads that her late husband Joe Scully had given her on their wedding day.

Joe had a little silver disc engraved with 'Joe loves Agnes' and had it fixed to the chain link that held the crucifix. She carried them everywhere in a silver cylinder case. They had been transferred from handbag to handbag more times than one could imagine. To travel without them, even on the shortest of journeys, would be something Agnes couldn't contemplate.

A year ago, while Agnes was out collecting her pension, she twisted her ankle on uneven paving. She went down like the proverbial ton of bricks, causing the contents of her handbag to spew out across the pavement. Her shoe abandoned her foot, her thick black stockings failed to protect her knees, while her stinging cheekbone leaked blood down her face. The weight of her body trapped her arm beneath her.

Fortunately, a passenger in a passing car noticed Agnes's crumpled body on the ground.

"Stop the car, John, stop the car!"

The woman ran to Agnes's aid, followed closely by her husband.

"John, ring the ambulance."

Agnes groaned. The last place she wanted to be taken to was the hospital.

"The ambulance won't be long Kate, they said they have one nearby."

"Can you tell me your name?" Kate said softly, as she stroked Agnes's forehead.

"I'm Agnes, well I was when I left home earlier. I'm not sure who I am now," she said with a little chuckle.

"Oh bless you, It's best you get checked over. You'll be fine." Kate reassured her.

John was busy recovering the contents of Agnes's handbag, including her pension book. He made sure the catch on her handbag was securely shut.

The ambulance arrived and with the skill the paramedics had learnt and practised many times before, they safely secured Agnes into the ambulance. Her weary eyes looked up at the paramedic.

"Where's my handbag?"

"It's here my love. Don't you worry. I'll make sure it stays with you in hospital. I'm Terry by the way. Just relax, we'll soon be there."

Lying in the gutter, near to where Agnes had her fall, lay her treasured rosary beads, still inside the silver cylinder case. It was nestled close to the kerbstone, which prevented it from being flattened by a passing vehicle. The sprays of wet dirt coated the beautiful silver case with a layer of silt. It lay there all night and at the same time Agnes lay in her hospital bed. She was content in the knowledge, or so she thought, that her rosary beads were safe inside her handbag, that had been carefully placed in her bedside locker. Having it close by allowed her to drift into a relaxing slumber.

The early morning sunrise warmed the earth, while that smell of freshness after rain filled the air. A lone pigeon perched on a nearby rooftop, cooing in contentment as the warmth from the sunshine filled his chest. In the distance, Harry, a part-time enthusiastic road sweeper, could be heard operating his machine deep into the gutter. The spinning brushes were creeping closer and closer to where Agnes's rosary beads lay.

In her hospital bed Agnes woke with a start.

My beads. She thought. *I want my rosary beads*.

At the exact same moment those spinning brushes of the road sweeper stopped abruptly. There lay the rosary beads, staring into the mouth of the diligent little sweeper, miraculously escaping its jaws. Harry was shocked his little machine had let him down, it was always so reliable. He bent down to see if anything was amiss. Nothing was apparent, but there glinting up at him was the cold, wet case of the rosary beads. Harry's usual finds were coins and the occasional bank note. He was a kind man and any money he found always went into a charity box. He was contented. His needs were simple. He lived by the law of gratitude. Harry opened the case and pulled out the beautiful rosary beads, allowing the sunlight to highlight the message: 'Joe loves Agnes'

Harry felt quite emotional. He knew these beads were very precious to someone and he would dearly love to know who.

Agnes had summoned the nurse to reach into her locker for her handbag. She frantically searched every compartment.

"My rosary beads." She wept. "Where are my rosary beads?"

The nurse noticed Agnes's distress and reminded her she was going home today.

"I am sure you will find them at home Agnes."

Agnes looked sternly at the nurse.

"I might be old, but I am certainly not stupid. My rosary beads are always secure in my handbag. I never go anywhere without them."

"There's always a first time Agnes. Always a first time." The nurse responded raising her eyebrow.

"I'll thank you kindly not to patronise me," Agnes replied as sharp as a pin.

An hour later the hospital transport had securely delivered Agnes back to the comfort of her own home. She usually spoke to Joe when she arrived home and told him where she had been. This time, however, she felt her own loneliness within the walls. Her coffee cup was still in the sink where she had left it before she had ventured out to collect her pension. There was no-one there to wash it up. There was just no-one there.

The loneliness hit her as hard as her fall. Although she hadn't wanted to go to hospital, it gave her the realisation that she missed having a good old chat. She and Joe used to have some good old chats.

She was exhausted, but she had to search her handbags for her rosary beads. She knew in her heart of hearts she was searching in vain, but for her own peace of mind it had to be done. She was right of course, she didn't find her beads.

The hospital had given her a clean bill of health, but she was quite bruised and achy. *Next week*, she thought, *when I feel less battered, I will put one of those postcards on the notice board in the post office, saying:*

Lost – Mother of Pearl Rosary Beads. If you find them please ring this number...

A week later Agnes did as she had planned and took her card to the post office. She handed it to Beryl, the stony faced, tight lipped post mistress, and politely asked her if she would pin it on the notice board. Beryl glanced down at the card with a haughty look.

"Well, it looks like there might not be a need for this."

Agnes looked puzzled. "But I want to ask if anyone has found my rosary beads".

"Yes, I know. There's a card on the board saying that someone has found rosary beads. There's a phone number to ring."

Agnes was so delighted, she was beside herself. She couldn't wait to get home to ring the number. She had to curtail her excitement and remind herself to walk with caution.

Agnes settled herself in her favourite chair with a cup of tea to hand. She unfolded the piece of paper on which the lovely Beryl had begrudgingly written down the phone number. She pressed the numbers on her extra large key pad, it rang several times before the answer machine kicked in. She wasn't prepared for that and had to think quickly.

"Oh. Err. I'm sorry to bother you, but I'm ringing about the rosary beads. Could you ring me back please?"

As soon as she ended the call, she realised she hadn't left her phone number.

"Oh dear Agnes, you are stupid at times," she said scolding herself.

She sat with the silence of her room, wondering if she should ring again. With that thought her phone rang.

"Hello" Agnes said softly.

"Hello my dear are you the lady that phoned about the rosary beads?"

"Yes I am. I'm sorry, I forgot to leave my phone number."

"Don't you worry about that, I have caller display. Now then, these rosary beads. They look really special to me and I want to make sure they are returned to the rightful owner. Would you mind describing them to me?"

"But of course not. They are mother of pearl and have a little disc by the crucifix saying 'Joe loves Agnes'. And I always keep them in a silver case."

"That's champion. Couldn't be better. I would be happy to drop them off to you."

"Well I live in Beaumont Avenue. Do you live near?"

"Ten minutes away. Would Sunday morning at 11am be ok? My name is Harry by the way."

"That would be perfect. My name is Agnes. That is so kind of you."

"No problem Agnes. I'll be with you on Sunday."

Agnes bought some best quality chocolate biscuits, the ones Joe used to like. Dead on the dot of 11am the chime of the doorbell filled the hallway. Agnes felt quite excited. She wasn't used to visitors, as she didn't have a family. It had only been her and Joe. It had only ever been her and Joe.

"Hello you must be Harry?"

"I am indeed and you must be Agnes?"

"Do come in Harry."

"Well, if you are sure."

"But of course. The least I can offer you for your kindness is a cup of tea and a biscuit."

"Well there's an offer I can't refuse. Thank you."

Agnes thought Harry had a very kind face and a beautiful demeanour. Harry produced the rosary beads from his pocket. He had put them in a little cloth pouch for extra protection. Agnes took them out of the case and placed a little kiss on the crucifix. Her eyes filled with tears.

"I can't thank you enough. You'll never know how grateful I am."

Harry explained how he found them and Agnes explained exactly how she lost them.

Over their tea and best chocolate biscuits, Agnes handed Harry a framed photo of Joe.

"This is my Joe."

"Oh, he looks a very handsome chap and by the message on your rosary beads, a very romantic chap."

"He was indeed. He always made me feel special. I do miss him. He's left a big void in my life."

"I do understand. I miss my Freda as well."

"I'm so sorry Harry. I have been wittering on about myself."

"No worries Agnes, you have been through a very emotional time recently. Opening up your heart and having a good chat probably helps you."

Agnes thought that was a very kind thing for Harry to say. It was nice to speak with someone who had an understanding.

"Well Agnes, it's been an absolute delight to meet you."

"You too Harry. You are a good listener."

"That's what my Freda used to say."

Harry walked down the hall towards the front door.

"Thank you for the tea and biscuits and don't forget to put one foot before the other when you are out and about."

Agnes laughed and thanked Harry again.

As she closed the door behind him, the silence hit her once more. She took the tea tray into the kitchen thinking it would be so lovely if Harry became a regular visitor. She so enjoyed his company and felt she'd known him for years.

Once again the chime of the doorbell filled the hallway. It surprised her to see Harry standing there.

"Hello Harry, did you forget something?"

"Well only to say Agnes, if you don't mind, I was wondering if I could visit again? I'm sure Joe and Freda wouldn't mind."

"Harry, that would be wonderful!"

Over the weeks their Sunday morning cups of tea extended to the cafe at the garden centre and even a trip to the cinema.

"Do you know Harry, a year or so ago, I thought my time on this earth was coming to an end. Now I feel like I have a new lease of life. Who would have thought, all those years ago, when my Joe gave me my wedding gift of rosary beads, they would lead to our beautiful friendship.

"Well, you know what they say about Him up there Agnes?"

"What's that Harry?"

"He moves in mysterious ways Agnes. He moves in mysterious ways."

5

Chance Encounter

Dorothy was looking despairingly out of her kitchen window. The rain was lashing against the glass, whilst the wind was weighing down the unpruned roses. It had been her intention to plant daffodil bulbs today.

Well that's my plans scuppered, she thought.

She was in desperate need of a new waterproof jacket and as the outerwear shop in the garden centre had an autumn sale on, she decided to go and see if she could grab herself a bargain.

Dorothy was a spinster. She did have a love in her life, many decades ago: Joe Byrne, of Irish descent, with striking Celtic looks, the black hair, blue eyes and bags of Irish charm. He was gentle and kind and loved her as every woman would want to be loved. He stole her heart, but never gave it back.

They first met on a misty autumn Wednesday afternoon, when Joe walked into the library where

Dorothy worked. His soft curls rolled across his forehead, his blue Irish eyes captivating. Dorothy looked up and asked Joe if she could help. Joe took a while to answer. He was fixated on her beautiful little nose, perfectly sprinkled with tiny freckles.

"Hi yes, I'd like to join please."

"Certainly sir. What name is it?"

"Err Joe. Joe Byrne."

Dorothy smiled at Joe. If ever there was a demonstration of love at first sight, that was it. She was entranced by the beauty of his hypnotic blue eyes, which seemed to be delving deeply into her soul. She had never seen such a beautiful specimen of human life.

Joe was studying at Nottingham university and became a regular visitor to the library, whether he needed to go or not. He wanted to ask Dorothy out, but he was a modest young man. He worried that if she rejected him he couldn't visit the library again. On his fourth visit he was returning a book. He hoped with all his heart Dorothy would be on duty. He had decided that if she was there, it was meant to be and he would ask her to join him for lunch on Saturday afternoon. As he was studying, he was living on a pretty tight budget and couldn't afford anywhere lavish and expensive. He knew she definitely worked on Wednesday afternoons.

When the next Wednesday came around he went in at precisely the same time as when he first saw her perfectly freckled little nose. The hinge on the library door always squeaked when it was opened. Dorothy heard the door, looked across and saw Joe. Her heart fluttered in her chest as she instantly made herself available at the counter. She smiled.

"Are you returning your book, or would you like to renew it?"

"I am returning it and in plenty of time, I can assure you. There are no fines to pay." Joe laughed clumsily.

"Well it would be nice if all our members were like you. Will that be all?"

Dorothy was cringing inside herself. *Will that be all? Will that be all? What else would he be expecting: cake and coffee?*

"Actually there is something," Joe stuttered "Would you be free to have lunch with me on Saturday afternoon?"

Dorothy blushed slightly. "That sounds lovely. Thank you Joe."

Inside she was screaming. *Of course I will! Of course I will!*

"Oh you remembered my name."

"Well it is on your card."

Of course I remembered your name, how could I forget, were the thoughts floating through her mind.

"How stupid of me, I had forgotten about my card. You know who I am, so can I ask your name?"

"I'm Dorothy."

That was the start of their beautiful romance. They were so in love and neither could imagine life without the other. Joe had come to call Dorothy 'his little Dotty' which made Dorothy feel even more special to Joe, if that was at all possible.

As the months passed by they had started to map out their future and couldn't wait to watch it gently unfold. Joe did have plans when he finished university and they didn't include Dorothy. He had planned with his lifelong friend Ben, to visit Ben's grandmother, who lived in the French Alps. Ben and Joe had planned to have a six month mental break to completely relax and unwind in the cool, clean air of the Alps. Joe had to break the news to Dorothy. He explained he couldn't let Ben down as they had planned this trip before starting university. Dorothy agreed with Joe.

"You must go Joe; Ben would be so disappointed if you didn't. Just promise me you will write."

"Oh my little Dotty, you don't even have to ask. Of course I will write to you."

Joe did write almost as soon as he got there. He then wrote a few days later. Dorothy began to love the sound of the letterbox. A letter from Joe only fell through her letterbox three times more. She never heard from him again.

Dorothy looked out of the window and noticed the rain had abated.

'*Right, time for me to make tracks to the garden centre.*' She thought.

She made a bee-line to the outdoor coats. Navy was her preferred colour. She felt it was a safe colour and always looked smart. There were three rails of clearance jackets, her trusted navy, khaki green and a striking cerise pink. The pink jacket unusually caught her eye. '*What a beautiful colour. I wonder if I dare wear it*'. She thought. As she picked it off the rail it was as if a lurking customer had read her thoughts.

"I think that pink would really suit you. I was looking at them myself, they are fantastic reductions."

Dorothy was taken by surprise. "Yes they are good reductions, but I have never had a pink coat," she laughed, "If I try it on would you give me your honest opinion?"

"Absolutely. I wouldn't tell you it looked nice on, if it didn't. Trust me."

Considering Dorothy had only met this lady five minutes earlier, she felt she could trust her. They had a really good connection.

Dorothy received a complimentary opinion about the coat and was rather surprised that she liked it too.

"Thank you so much for your help with my coat. I did appreciate it. Looks like I will be wearing my first ever pink coat. Actually I was going to the cafe for a cup of tea. Would you like to join me? I'm Dorothy by the way."

"Well I have nothing to go home for. Thank you so much, that would be very nice. And I'm Barbara."

The two women chatted away with such ease, almost as if they were lifelong friends.

"Do you live far, Dorothy?"

"No, not far, in Sherwood Avenue if you know it. I used to have a little flat in town, but that was a lifetime ago."

"You're joking. I live in Cramworth Grove. We are practically neighbours. You must come for coffee."

The two women had struck up a friendship and enjoyed each other's company, so much so, that when Christmas came around Barbara invited Dorothy for Christmas dinner.

Dorothy noticed there was an extra place setting.

"Will there be another guest joining us Barbara?

No Dorothy. It's for my husband, John. I am a widow. I always set him a place."

I'm sorry Barbara, I had no idea. It's a lovely thing to do. I just always thought you were a spinster like me."

The women had never discussed their marital status. Dorothy never discussed Joe. She carried her heartache deep within and never shared her memories of her beloved Joe with anyone. Her love for him today is even greater than when she first met him. If the truth be known she lived in constant hope, that one day, Joe would turn up, despite her moving out of her little flat, where Joe had been a frequent visitor.

Likewise Barbara never talked about her husband. She was a private person and dealt with issues alone. Although for the first time, she felt she had found in Dorothy someone she could talk to.

"Barbara that was a delicious lunch, thank you so much. Now I insist on washing up."

"And I insist it all goes in the dishwasher. It doesn't get used too much with me being on my own, so it could do with a spin."

"OK. I submit." Dorothy laughed.

"Actually Dorothy, I like to visit the cemetery on Christmas day. Just to take some flowers for John. Would you like to come with me and then we could go for a constitutional walk in the park?"

"Only if you are sure you would like me to come. I don't want to intrude."

"You wouldn't be intruding Dorothy. For the first time I wouldn't be facing the emotional loneliness on my own."

On the short drive to the cemetery Barbara told Dorothy she met John when she was nursing

"We are here now. John is just on the edge of the cemetery."

The two women walked slowly to where John lay. The cold afternoon air was starting to bite. You could see it leaving their lungs as they spoke.

"Barbara I'll give you five minutes," Dorothy said, as she sat down on a nearby bench.

She watched as Barbara took a crumpled tissue from her pocket to dab her tears and at the same time cleared away a few pieces of windblown litter. Dorothy stood up from the bench, she walked towards Barbara as she felt she needed a hug. She placed her arm around Barbara's shoulder and gave it a little squeeze.

"Are you ok? Your flowers look lovely Barbara."

Dorothy lifted her head to read the gravestone. Her eyes became paralysed. The blood drained from her body. Her legs weakened as she fainted to the ground. The gravestone read 'Rest In Peace Joe Byrne'.

Barbara was alarmed and bent down.

"Dorothy are you ok?"

She was slowly coming round.

"Yes I'm ok. I just had a dizzy turn. Must be this cold air."

"Come on we had better get you back and I'll make you a nice cup of hot chocolate. If you are very good I'll add a drop of brandy."

"I'm sorry Barbara I didn't mean to interrupt your time with Jo... err John.

"No worries. I expect you are wondering why his headstone says Joe."

"Well yes, but I didn't like to ask."

"I'll tell you Dorothy. When I first saw John in hospital he was in a coma and remained in that state for six months. He had been in a nasty car accident with his friend Ben. Ben sadly died. Some idiot hit them head on, on a sharp mountainous bend. John had head injuries and was paralysed from the waist down. There was another Joe on the ward, so I called my Joe, John and I continued to call him John. Oh you should have seen him Dorothy, he was beautiful. He had gorgeous black curls, blue eyes and such a warm smile, despite all of his injuries. We became the best of friends. I fell in love with him at first sight and he was fond of me. I knew it wasn't anymore than that. He told me there was someone in his life with whom he was totally in love. I did offer to help him get in touch with her, but he was adamant that no-one would want a paralysed partner. He needed twenty four hour care. I loved him so much I was willing to play second best to his little Dotty, as he called her. You could say we had a marriage of friendship and convenience. That's it really Dorothy. You now know my life story. Thank you for listening so patiently."

The tears were rolling down Dorothy's cheeks. She could see her Joe in her mind's eye, his soft curls, blue eyes and his wonderful gentle smile. Her love for him now is as immense as it was all those years ago. How she wished she could hold him once more.

"I didn't mean to upset you Dorothy." Barbara said gently.

"It was such a sad story. Thank you so much for sharing. You'll never know how much that meant to me."

Dorothy always knew that somehow Joe would come back to her.

6

Loneliness

The fire crackled in the grate. The smell of roasting turkey filled the house. Outside snow was gently falling, arriving like an unexpected visitor that you never knew how long they would stay. Doreen Collins watched with delight as her parents and children opened their presents. She adored giving presents.

"Another sherry Mum?"

"Ooo our Doreen, don't mind if I do. It is Christmas after all."

Doreen was watching through her spectacles of yesteryear, bringing back memories of over thirty years ago on Christmas day. The stark reality was that she was sitting alone looking out of the window.

There was no exchanging of presents, glasses of sherry, or the smell of roasting turkey. There was just a microwave dinner for one, waiting to be pierced and pinged at the appropriate time before the Queen's speech.

Visitors were arriving at neighbours' houses. Excited children running up the driveway of next door to greet their grandparents. Across the road, Mrs. King's daughter arriving to take her mum back to her home for dinner. Mr. Green's grandson had come to fetch him. Doreen watched as the grandson steadied Mr. Green and led him safely to the car. He carefully fastened his grandfather's seat belt. She could see the cold air with each breath they took. The exhaust fumes spewed out and merged into the fogginess of the day as the ignition turned on. The car slowly moved down Mr. Green's drive, the headlights shone across into Doreen's window. *I would loved to be picked up,* thought Doreen. She turned away from the window, to her empty room. She had taken off her spectacles of yesteryear and gently wiped her tears that had fallen down her cheeks.

Doreen had two daughters, Josephine and Amelia. Josephine had two children, but lived in Australia with her husband Tim. Doreen adored her grandchildren and their absence from her life made her heart ache. She hadn't seen them for five years.

Amelia was married to Sam. They didn't have children. Amelia always made her obligatory visit to Doreen a week before Christmas. Doreen hated being an obligation. Amelia would tell her mother that her job as a solicitor was so busy and all she wanted to do was to slob out on the sofa over the Christmas break.

Doreen pulled her armchair nearer the fire. She lifted the poker, pulled back the fireguard and gave the coals a little poke, to liven them up. She watched the sparks as they flew up the chimney. She could feel the heat warming her body and wondered how her Christmas days and indeed all her days, had become so lonely. She couldn't remember when she became redundant as chief cook. She did know her job was still vacant, as no-one had filled the vacancy to cook for her.

She walked into the kitchen, the sound of piercing the film wrap over her meal seemed louder than it should be inside the empty walls. She took her dinner for one on a tray to eat in front of the fire. She turned on the television at precisely the same time as the Queen started to deliver her speech.

She won't be alone, thought Doreen. *Truth be known, she will probably have more family than she can cope with. Oh I'd love to be Queen for a day, Christmas day.*

When the strains of the National Anthem were filling the room, Doreen's eyes were gently closing. Twenty minutes later she woke abruptly as her tray started to slide off her lap. Her reflexes were good, she caught it in time, with just a knife plunging over the edge.

Doreen entered the kitchen and cleared away what little there was to clear. She returned to her sitting room and stretched out on the sofa to continue her slumber. Sleeping was her way of escaping from her loneliness.

She woke around 6pm. The last light of the day had truly disappeared. The bright light of the moon lit up the night sky, illuminating the snow beneath. The car tracks made earlier in the soft snow were now hard, icy little ditches glinting under a Christmas moon. Doreen walked to the window taking a last look at Christmas day. The only sign of life was a stray cat walking across her lawn, leaving evidence of its visit by little paw prints indented in the snow. *It must be so cold, but it doesn't seem to mind.* She pulled her green velvet curtains together, making sure they met in the middle, with no gaps at all. She turned and once again looked into the emptiness of her room, knowing there wasn't a soul in the world whom she cared about, who was thinking about her.

"Well it's been a long day Doreen. Do you fancy a mince pie and a nice cup of tea?"

Those were the first words she had spoken all day and she was the only person there to hear them.

7

Regrets

Robert Morris rose early that Saturday morning in April. He was a night owl, so it was unusual for him to relinquish his duvet before 10am. He was expecting some deliveries of wine and books, his two favourite pastimes. He wanted to make sure he was up and about in case the courier made an early morning appearance. What he didn't want was for his deliveries to be left with neighbours. Robert wasn't a sociable animal; in fact one could say he was a loner.

He did have one close friend, John Cavendish. They were both chess enthusiasts and got together once a week to do battle on the chess board.

Robert proceeded to unlock his front porch. His parcels were left there if he failed to hear the door bell.

He was a man in his late 60s. He had full mobility and plenty of hobbies to keep him occupied. Although a bachelor, he once had a love in his life that had remained the love of his life, to the exclusion of all others. They met in their late 20s, when he joined the staff of a Derbyshire accountancy firm where she worked. The touch paper was lit; it was love at first sight. When they met, she was Heidi Hemmingway, soon to become Heidi Carter. Her wedding was arranged: the church, the cars, the cake, the flowers and all the other ingredients required to unite a man and woman in holy matrimony. That was of course all before she met Robert.

In their clandestine meetings over the next few months, they declared their love for each other. Heidi knew she was past the point of no return and her wedding had to go ahead. She could not put her parents through the stressful ordeal of calling the whole thing off.

Heidi's mother was very highly strung and would look upon Heidi's actions as a disgrace to the family and a total embarrassment. It was all about what other people thought, as far as Mrs. Hemmingway was concerned.

On Saturday 24 September 1960, Heidi Hemmingway became Heidi Carter.

Robert was heartbroken and turned into the unsociable loner that he remained for the rest of his life. He was desperately seeking employment elsewhere. Fleetingly seeing Heidi at work and occasionally having his nostrils filled with her perfume as he walked down a corridor that she had walked five minutes previously, was literally draining him. He could hide his emotions inwardly, but his broken heart was displaying in his physical self. Flesh was leaving his body, allowing his clothes to hang more freely than before. He was a stranger to the shower cubicle, leaving his straight dark hair matted with grease. His colleagues were showing concern as they assumed he must be ill; there was no prescription to heal his broken heart.

It was a Monday morning and two months since Heidi's wedding. Heidi walked into her supervisor's office and handed in her notice. Her husband had been promoted, which relocated him to Scotland.

Robert handled the news with a conflicted mind. It would mean that his precious Heidi would leave his life for good. The alternative would be to see her occasionally in the workplace, around the town and at Mass on Sundays. Robert couldn't continue with the latter and knew if there was any chance of him salvaging his own life, Heidi's move was for the best. Heidi did make the move to Scotland and walked out of Robert's life for good.

The afternoon was turning chilly and the threatening rain clouds were darkening the sky. Robert's parcels had been delivered, but the careless delivery man had left the porch door ajar. Jack, a vigilant neighbour, although some called him nosey, was out walking his dog. He noticed Robert's parcels, but more importantly he noticed the door was ajar. Jack knew everybody's movements. He lived opposite Robert and knew that on the days that Robert didn't even want to exchange pleasantries with the delivery man, he would purposely not answer the door, so the parcels would be left in the porch. He also knew, as soon as the coast was clear, Robert would immediately retrieve his parcels. Jack saw that the parcels were still there some five hours later. That in itself alerted him to be concerned, especially as Robert's car was on the drive and hadn't moved all day. Jack proceeded to walk up the drive. He rang the doorbell several times. The house was in complete silence. There wasn't a glimmer of light escaping from any nook or cranny. Jack pulled the porch door closed and immediately returned home to ring the police. Twenty minutes later Jack went out to meet them. He was in his element of being chief informant, even if there wasn't too much to inform.

The police officer called out. "Hello, hello. Mr Morris. Are you there?"

There was still complete silence. One of the officers walked to the back of the house and peered through the French doors of the living room. There he was, Mr. Robert James Morris, lying face down on the badly stained unhoovered carpet. The officer immediately ran to the front of the house and gained entry. Sadly Robert had passed away some hours ago.

At the Sunday Mass before Robert's funeral on Wednesday, the priest read out the notifications for the week. On reading the details of the funeral Father Michael added a request. He asked the congregation if they would be so kind to attend Robert's funeral, if time allowed. He explained that Robert didn't have a family and few friends.

There was one person in the congregation for whom time did allow. That person was Heidi Carter, nee Hemmingway. She had divorced her husband five years after their marriage. She knew it was a sham, on her part anyway. She realised Robert was, and still is, the love of her life. She moved back to the area after retiring from her job in Scotland. She moved to a neighbouring town, but still attended the same church that she and Robert had attended all those years ago, in the hope that she would see him again. Her hopes were in vain, as Robert had turned his back on his faith the day Heidi married. He couldn't forgive God for allowing such a love to enter his life and then take it away.

Father Michael's words regarding the news of Robert's death echoed in her mind. Her sadness, her pain, her heartache and her regrets were overwhelming. The hope that she carried within drained from her body. *If only I had put myself first,* she thought, as hot salty tears ran down her cheeks. Inside her heart was screaming, but she couldn't let it out into the silence of the church.

The day of the funeral had arrived. Despite Robert being a private, lonely man his funeral was well supported. The parishioners had done him proud. John Cavendish, his friend and opponent in chess, came to pay his last respects, along with Jack, the vigilant neighbour, who was as 'vigilant' as ever.

The lone figure of Heidi Carter sat behind the rest of the congregation carrying a single red rose.

John Cavendish was the only person in whom Robert confided. John knew all about Heidi and the clandestine meetings. John was a good listener and someone who would keep your secrets safe. That was all that Robert could have hoped for.

Heidi's thoughts went back to her wedding day. She relived the moments she walked up this very same aisle and promised words of commitment that she knew she couldn't keep - and all to keep her mother happy.

Now Robert had made the same journey to the altar, but a journey Heidi wished she didn't have to witness.

How Great Thou Art echoed around the walls. Heidi's tears turned into silent sobs. Robert had stipulated this hymn in his will. He had fallen out with God, but hadn't abandoned his faith entirely.

John Cavendish took his place at the lectern. He gave a short eulogy to celebrate Robert's life, making it light-hearted by joking that they had a game of chess to finish.

John walked back to his seat and observed the lonely figure of Heidi, realising straight away who she was.

Heidi couldn't breathe. She wanted to tell the congregation that Robert was a beautiful and kind man, whom she had never stopped loving.

The Mass ended. Heidi couldn't believe what she was hearing. As Robert's coffin was carried out, it was accompanied by the beautiful, haunting sound of Vaughan Williams, *The Lark Ascending.* It was such a special piece of music for them. Robert gave Heidi a recording of it the week before she married. He asked her to promise that she would always think of him when she heard it. Little did he know she would be hearing it at his funeral.

Heidi's lone figure followed the procession out into the graveyard. *I denied Robert once*, she thought. *And I am not going to deny him any longer.* As the coffin was lowered, Heidi walked forward and placed her red rose with Robert, which signified her love for him.

Human nature being what it is, people wondered who Heidi was, especially as they had been told

Robert didn't have a family and few friends. Jack the vigilant neighbour, was beside himself with curiosity. John Cavendish remained silent, the loyal friend right to the end and beyond.

8

Where There's A Will

His bones felt brittle with cold, his joints stiff and muscles tight with pain. Starvation hollowed his stomach and dehydration pounded inside his skull. The rain was unforgiving, washing pieces of disintegrating cardboard towards the overflowing gutters. The small doorway of Betty's Boutique provided insufficient shelter for George Harper, as he curled up like a hibernating hedgehog to avoid the lashing rain.

His usual abode was a narrow, uninterrupted covered alleyway that led to the rear of a graveyard. George was surprised to see his hide-a-way had been occupied by another lost soul that night.

He hadn't always slept rough; he didn't need to. His life had been as near perfect as it could be. He was a highly regarded teacher, with a lovely comfortable home in the countryside and, to complete the picture, he had a beautiful wife and child.

Sadly two years ago, on a dark November night, their home was destroyed by fire and neither Lisa,

George's wife, nor Sean their son had survived. George was on duty at a parents' evening at his school. Some of the teachers went to the pub afterwards and George uncharacteristically joined them. That was, and still is to this day, his biggest regret. 'What ifs' have circled his head ever since.

"What if I had been at home," he would say. "I might have saved them."

"What if I hadn't gone to the pub, I might have saved them."

The 'what ifs' were unrelenting, they haunted him day and night. He had lost everything. He withdrew inside himself. His emotional pain was so intense he didn't want to live. George moved 50 miles away and made the pavements and alleyways of the city of Leeds his home.

After a night in the doorway of Betty's Boutique he knew he must arrive early at his abode at the rear of the graveyard, which in comparison seemed almost five star.

He never sought help at hostels or shelters; his mental state, with depression and hopelessness, wouldn't allow it. Thankfully his covered alleyway was free and mercifully the night was dry and still. He had managed to find some out-of-date sandwiches and snacks behind a local supermarket. His thoughts, as always, were of his beautiful family. He was remembering one of

Lisa's sayings: "Where there's a will, there's a way." she would say.

She was nearly always right, as she had the will and always found a way, something George really admired in her.

"I wonder if she would say that to me now," he thought.

What he did know was that he would tell her he didn't have a will, so how could he find a way. On those bitter sweet reflections George let his tired body take control and lead him into deep sleep.

Next morning George woke feeling his black cloud of depression had lifted slightly, but couldn't understand why. Then he remembered that Lisa had come to him in a dream and told him to walk in the graveyard. George was really rock bottom, so had nothing to lose by following his dream. As he entered the graveyard, the day was blessed with sunshine and the melodic sound of birdsong greeted him. He sat on a bench wondering what he was doing there. *It was only a dream*, he thought, *only a dream*. He had kept some of his out of date snacks for breakfast. A friendly robin decided to join him. As hungry as George was, he couldn't deprive the robin of breakfast, so generously shared it with his new feathered friend. Out of the blue a voice was heard,

"Ah, I see you're feeding the birds."

It was the vicar from the church. George looked startled and anxious; he had lost the art of conversation. The vicar could see George looked dishevelled and was perceptive enough to know that George was a troubled man.

"Would you like to come into the vicarage for breakfast? I'm Paul by the way."

George shocked himself by accepting Paul's kind invitation. An hour later and George had confided his life. That was down to the wonderful listening skills of Paul. He had the ability to give complete strangers the confidence and trust to pour out their hearts.

"George would you help me?"

"Help you, how can I help you?"

"Well, believe it or not, I heard your devastating news at the time. I have a close friend who is a vicar in your parish. I want to start classes for the homeless and under-privileged and I need a teacher. I have a spare room, plenty of food and my wife is a very good cook, so you can sing for your supper." Paul laughed and even coaxed a smile from George. George was astounded. He was astounded at Paul's offer and astounded that he actually accepted. He was so overcome, he wept. Two years of silent grief came flooding out of him.

"Let it out my friend, let it out." Paul laid his hand on George's shoulder.

"Just always remember one thing George."

"What's that Paul?"

"Where there's a will, there's a way."

Tears rolled down George's cheeks as he lifted his eyes to heaven and whispered, "Thank you Lisa for restoring my will and helping me find my way."

9

A Weekend Away

John and Maggie Brennan were woken Monday to Friday at six am. by the high shrill of their alarm clock. It was for this reason that they refused to get up before 10am. on Saturdays, except for one of them to go and make a cup of tea and hurriedly get back to the warmth and comfort of the duvet.

However, this Saturday was different. They had to be at their local car showroom for 10am. John was excited as he was taking receipt of a brand new Audi. He had never had a current year number plate before. Maggie was equally excited, as her car was being traded in and she was having John's old Audi. Maggie didn't know much about cars, but she liked the sound of Audi. She thought it sounded posh.

They arrived at the showroom ten minutes before their appointment time, signed all the necessary paperwork before Maggie oohed and aahed over the flowers on the back seat.

To drive the short distance back home was not going to happen. New Audi will travel. They drove to their nearest shopping park and picked up some nice food for the weekend. John was enjoying playing with his new toy so much, they decided to move on and drive to a country pub for lunch. John parked the car as far away from the entrance that was possible. He was already becoming paranoid that someone might scratch his new prize possession. There was a definite nip in the air as they walked across the car park. The sight of a table for two next to a real fire added even more pleasure to their day.

John worked in the accounts department of a large manufacturing company in the Midlands. He was an auditor, but he wasn't dull, as the general opinion of auditors suggests. In fact he was quite the opposite. He was lively, interesting and definitely had charisma and charm. He could add his penny worth or two to most conversations, yet still had the ability to be a good listener. Maggie worked as a dental nurse. She wasn't quite as lively and charismatic as John, but she was very caring and good natured.

After their pub lunch, on the drive back home, John surprised Maggie by saying, "Forgot to mention Maggie, but I will be away next weekend. Been invited to a stag 'do'."

"But you hate a stag 'do'."

"I know. It's a young lad in wages. He hasn't been with us long and he's new to the area, so I think I should make the effort."

"Well, don't come moaning to me after, saying how much you hated it. Where is it anyway?"

"Err, hmm, Bristol. Yes that's where it is Bristol. I think he used to live there. We are going down on Friday straight after work and coming back Sunday after breakfast. We will probably need a nice greasy fry up." John laughed.

As the week went on Maggie was relishing the thought of having the weekend to herself, although it would have been John's turn to venture out from the warmth of the duvet and make a cup of tea. As that wasn't going to happen, Maggie rose as usual, indulged in a lazy breakfast while listening to her favourite radio station: Radio 4. Lazing around for too long wasn't really her style. After deliberating between the pile of ironing that was staring at her from the basket perched on the washing machine, or cleaning her new car, she opted for the latter.

John never kept a tidy car; Maggie always called it his office. There was so much paperwork stuffed into every available pocket. She did appreciate John removing the offending items before she became the proud owner. The paperwork was the only thing he removed, scuff marks and muddy car mats still remained.

Donned in a worn out old track suit and armed with her hand hoover, white vinegar and spray polish, Maggie made her way out to her car, like a soldier going into battle. After an hour had passed, windows were sparkling, car mats were as black as coal and scuff marks had faded into oblivion. She was standing back praising herself for the excellent job she had done, when she suddenly remembered she hadn't hoovered the door wells.

Knowing John, she thought, *they are probably an inch deep in sandwich crumbs.*

Placing the thin nozzle attachment inside the door, there was a heavy suction sound. It was an envelope containing a piece of paper that had escaped John's clear out. Lifting the letter from the envelope Maggie was surprised to read that is was a confirmation letter from a hotel in Brighton. It was confirming a reservation for a Mr. and Mrs. Brennan for a double room and it was for the very same weekend that John had gone to Bristol. Maggie felt sick, her head was spinning.

"Stay calm Maggie, stay calm," she whispered to herself.

She went inside to shower and decided she would ring her very best friend Rachel. Maggie had complete trust in Rachel and was the only person she confided in; they were always there for each other through thick and thin.

Rachel will make me feel better. She always does.

As she rang her mobile it went straight to voice mail. Maggie's heart sank. She then tried her landline. Rachel's husband Sean answered. He had a lovely warm Dublin accent, which Maggie found so comforting.

"How you doing Maggie?"

"Sean, is Rachel there?"

"No, she's gone to Brighton on a hen weekend. I thought you knew. She is travelling back after breakfast on Sunday."

10

Robbie

Nurses were leaving their shifts. Patient visiting time was coming to an end. Outside, coughing came from cold air entering warm lungs.

Nurse Jean McKenzie was rushing home as she was going out partying to celebrate Burns Night with her husband Andrew. Her sister Clare should have been joining them, but she had rung Jean the day before to say she was feeling under the weather, so she would be giving the Burns Night a miss.

Clare had been working away as a live in nanny, but her three year placement had come to an end. She had returned to her flat, which was a couple of miles away from Jean. Clare had decided to take some time off before applying for another position as a nanny, but hopefully not living in this time, as she really wanted to have more of a home life of her own.

Jean McKenzie had been late that morning and had managed to squeeze her car on the edge of the car park, next to the shrubbery. She flicked her key fob. Her car let out a squeak. The lights came on, as if to greet her. As Jean placed her bag in the boot of her car she was wishing she could go home and luxuriate in a hot bath and slip into her pyjamas. A Burns Night party was the last thing she needed after a long shift. With a deep sigh she banged the boot shut. The noise of the boot disturbed a cat lurking in the shrubbery. Jean hated cats and hoped it wouldn't present itself to her, before she made it into her car. Jean was like a magnet to cats, whether it be at friends' houses, or even in her own garden.

"Oh my God, there it goes again."

The cold damp night air had placed a veil of mist over the car windows. She grabbed a cloth from inside of the passenger door. She quickly cleared the glass with her bright blue micro-fibre cloth. After wrestling with the shrubbery she managed to install herself into her car.

How did I get out of this car? She thought.

She started the ignition and wound down the window to clear her wing mirror. The cat exercised its vocals once more.

"Sorry Mr. Cat you can't get me now," she laughed.

As her window reached shut Jean realised the cat hadn't stopped crying this time. She thought it sounded more like the cry of a baby. Her eyes widened as she gasped loudly, "no it can't be."

She opened her window again.

If that's a cat, then I'm Lady Gaga.

She searched for the torch in her glove compartment and shone it into the shrubbery. She could see a white mound. She moved the car forward to enable her to get out easier and take a closer look.

The white mound was indeed a white carrier bag, which seemed to be moving. Jean carefully placed her hand under the bag and gently lifted it towards her.

"Oh my word. You're not a cat at all. Come on my little sweetheart, let's get you in the warm."

Jean always carried a large cardigan in her car for those 'just in case' moments. If this wasn't a 'just in case' moment, she didn't know what was. Her cardigan was adequate enough to wrap around this precious little soul several times. Holding her small bundle securely, but very gently, she eventually reached the Maternity block.

Jean frantically summoned a couple of nurses. They gathered around her excitedly, as if it was she who had given birth. The baby was taken to a small room. The white carrier bag was carefully cut away. The tiny body was wrapped in a fleecy blanket, which was removed to enable a thorough examination.

"Oh it's a boy. Let's call him Robbie. It is Burns Night after all."

The two nurses and the doctor they had called thought the name was very appropriate. Despite his ordeal Robbie seemed to be a bonny healthy baby.

"Oh my God it's Burns Night and I should be at a party. Andrew will be wondering where I am!" Jean exclaimed

She quickly left the ward and phoned Andrew to explain. They decided that they were both too tired for partying and agreed to be party poopers together and stay at home with a take-a-way.

In a few days time, at the end of the month, Jean was finishing work. She desperately wanted a baby and thought her stressful job and late night shifts were jeopardising her ability to conceive. Jean and Andrew had even set the wheels in motion to adopt, as they wanted a family come what may.

The next morning Jean rang her sister Clare to see how she was feeling and to tell her of the eventful evening the night before. Jean dialled Clare's number. It took a while for her to answer and she knew by the sound of Clare's voice that she was still under the weather.

"Oh dear Clare, you sound a bit rough. Are you ok?"

"Yeah I'll be fine, just not one hundred per cent. Probably a bug."

"Clare, you'll never guess what happened to me last night!"

Jean proceeded to tell the full story of finding baby Robbie.

"I want to pop into Maternity before my shift tonight and see how the little bairn is getting on. I must go Clare, someone's at the door. Look after yourself."

Clare sat staring at the floor. She looked pale with dark shadows under her eyes, emphasising her pallor even more. She picked up a half drunk mug of coffee. She cupped her hands around the mug, to salvage the remaining heat. Hot salty tears ran down her cheeks blurring out the blood stained rug that lay at her feet. How she wished her tears could wash away the past twenty four hours. Her mind was haunted by the catastrophic vision that was etched in her memory.

She couldn't erase the sight of the white plastic carrier bag as she carefully placed it in the shrubbery. It was alive, and it was alive with the life of her new born son. She hadn't noticed Jean's car parked nearby. Everything was a blur. With her hoody covering most of her face and heart beating hard in her chest, she hurriedly made her way back to her car, which seemed a million miles away. Despite the cold night, her body was clammy with sweat. Her legs were heavy, yet paradoxically felt like jelly. Her car came into view through the murky mist of the night air. It was parked illegally on a grass verge well away from the main car park. Her hands were shaking as she fumbled for her keys. Her chest was burning and she wanted to throw up.

"Come on Clare hold yourself together, before you pass out."

She drove herself back to her flat, but couldn't recall a thing about the journey. Her weary traumatised body climbed the stairs. She fell in through the door. Making her way to the bedroom, she collapsed on the bed. Her sobbing was so intense, it exhausted her physical and emotional state even further, pushing her into deep sleep.

The next evening Jean arrived at Maternity an hour before her shift started. Baby Robbie was just about to have his feed. Jean put in a very polite request asking if she could feed Robbie.

"Ok. We could do with a spare pair of hands."

Nurse tested the heat of the milk on the back of her hand before handing him to Jean.

"Keep the bottle held up, so the teat is always full. He won't gulp in any air that way."

"Yes nurse", Jean joked, while making a salute at the same time.

She couldn't take her eyes off this little bundle of loveliness. Baby Robbie lifted his arm and snuggled his tiny mouth around the teat. Feeling content he lowered his little arm and rested his hand on Jeans. His tiny fingers flexed in and out onto Jean's hand as he fed. Her heart melted. She had no doubt that finishing work to start a family was exactly what she wanted. However, she did have mixed emotions. Nursing was her love, but having a baby was her longing and it was the longing that won the battle.

Six weeks had passed. Jean and Andrew had both had confirmation that they were biologically healthy enough to conceive.

Clare was over the moon as her agency had found her a post as a nanny. It was local, which didn't require her to live in. She was looking forward to getting back to normal life after her ordeal. However, she was feeling some trepidation as the child was virtually a new born baby. Her hopes were that she would have the emotional strength to hold herself together.

Leaving her job had given Jean a new lease of life. She was less tense and even enjoyed homemaking. Going for a swim in the afternoons was a real luxury. In her previous life, if she wasn't working a shift she was sleeping. She was convinced that the new calm relaxed Jean would soon be pregnant. In the meantime, if they had the opportunity to adopt, both Jean and Andrew would be happy with that also. She had heard it wasn't unusual for couples to adopt and then conceive naturally.

The morning had arrived for Clare to take up her new post as Nanny for Sheila King. Sheila King worked as an accountant from the basement of her large Victorian home. This arrangement was so convenient for Sheila and for Clare. Clare had visited the house the previous week to familiarise herself with the logistics of her nannying duties. The wee bairn had been out with his granny for a pram ride in the park. So Clare didn't actually meet him.

Clare had a five mile journey to her new place of work, which pleased her immensely. After her recent trauma Clare felt safer working closer to home. Being able to call in on her sister for a cup of tea and a chat was a massive bonus. Her emotional and psychological state was still quite fragile. Knowing she could see Jean for a sisterly hug was so reassuring.

Clare tentatively rang the doorbell. There was a knot in her stomach. Her mind fleetingly caught a glimpse of her traumatic ordeal on Burns Night. She shook her head to delete the image. Sheila King opened the door.

"Hello Clare, nice to see you again. You'll be pleased to know he's asleep at the moment, so you can make yourself a nice hot drink. Granny went back yesterday. I think she was worn out." Sheila laughed.

Clare gave a little false laugh in reply.

"Right Clare! Can I leave you to it? I have a client at 10am and I have to get some papers ready."

"Yes you carry on Sheila. I'll just wash my hands and pop up to the nursery."

Clare pushed open the nursery door. Her heart was pounding. She looked in the cot and saw this perfect, beautifully formed specimen of life: from his tiny rosebud mouth, to the long dark eye lashes that rested gently on his silky smooth skin. Her mind flashed back to the white carrier bag she had placed in the shrubbery. She was in utter disbelief of her actions on that dreadful night. She sat herself down, inhaled deep breaths and exhaled with a slow release of air. She knew her emotional state wouldn't heal overnight and she also knew that this wee bairn, who lay sleeping in his cot before her, had been entrusted to her care. And that's exactly what she was going to do.

Clare had the weekends off. She felt emotionally drained after her first week, so took the opportunity of a luxurious lie in on Saturday morning. She was woken by a phone call. It was Jean.

"Hello Clare. How are you doing? Haven't seen you for ages. How do fancy coming over for Sunday lunch and a catch up? I also have something to show you."

Clare accepted the invitation. In fact she couldn't think of anything else she would rather do.

She arrived at Jeans about mid-day on Sunday. She gave Jean a big tight hug, mainly because it was Clare that needed the hug.

"Gosh something smells nice. Are we having lamb?" Clare asked.

"Yes we are, but dinner will be another hour yet. Anyway I have a surprise for you before we eat."

Jean disappeared upstairs. Within minutes she was back holding a baby with Andrew by her side.

"I have been bursting to tell you Clare, we adopted this little one last week, but the biggest surprise is that he is Robbie, who I found in the shrubbery on Burns Night. Say hello to your nephew."

11

Conversations

Don't you just love to eavesdrop on conversations? You can be anywhere: restaurants, buses, trains, although maybe not trains, as you don't have to eavesdrop: you have no choice, especially if a mobile phone is present. You can guarantee the first line of conversation will be "I'm on the train". That's neither stimulating, nor inspiring.

I like the meaty ones, the ones that tell a story, but I don't know the full story, yet. I only pick up snippets. I put them aside in a corner of my brain, waiting for the next tasty morsel to be tossed out. When I have sufficient snippets, I start to piece them together, like a pictureless jigsaw. Sometimes I get the whole story, all the juicy gossip, all the details, the whole picture. Or sometimes I add a morsel of my own. I think that's allowed, if it enriches the story. That is what I call a very satisfying eavesdropping session, so the jigsaw can now be complete.

There are, of course, the gossip informants, who are very guarded. They are aware of eavesdroppers like myself. Quite happily they tell their news to their audience, but when it comes to the heart of the matter, the bit you can sink your teeth into, the very piece you wanted to hear, they draw in their listeners closer, to signal it is for their ears only and not to be repeated. I know very well, the very same story, with a few embellishments, will fall from their lips in a few days time, to a different audience of listeners. As for myself, I love to hear the gossip, but I never repeat it, except through my stories of course.

12

The Bench

There were some nights when Marian Nolan found that sleep wouldn't come easy to her. She lay in the dark and stillness of the night. She was unhappy, her thoughts circled round in her mind. She never felt she mattered to her family and certainly didn't feel loved. However, if favours were needed it was good old dependable Marian who had the honour to be asked, and she never said "no." Maybe that was her problem. She always said, "The more you do for people, the less they think of you." In her case she was right. She longed for love and affection, but didn't get any, even from her husband David. She was the butt of his jokes and he loved to get cheap laughs at her expense. Marian never used to mind and even joined in with the laughs, but it was becoming constant and it drained her. Her life was so unhappy in every area. She was worried about her catastrophic thoughts. She wanted to commit suicide, but she didn't want to die. She was desperate for those close to her to know how she felt. Family was everything to her, but she was never included, to the point of being ignored.

Marian was a strong woman and some days she could talk herself out of her sadness. She would distract herself by mooching around charity shops looking for a good novel. On one particular day she was in her favourite charity shop. She noticed there had been the addition of a tall stand holding various cards and some beautiful bookmarks. She stopped to read the bookmarks as they had lovely quotes from various authors. There was one that really resonated with her and gave her that light bulb moment. It was a quote from the author George Eliot and it read, *"It is never too late to be what you might have been."*

Suddenly, within a few seconds, she had clarity in her mind. She realised she was wasting her life worrying and caring about people who didn't value her. She also realised it was no use criticising people for treating her badly, when she also treated herself badly, by letting their bad behaviour take its toll on her. It was now time for her to be what she might have been.

Marian did have lots of interests, but writing short stories was something she used to love to do. Now was the time to stop wasting her energy on useless thoughts. Instead, she would direct it down the creative path and rekindle her love of short story writing.

Before returning home Marian called into a stationers to purchase a nice big notebook and some new biros. She liked to handwrite her stories, as that allowed her to take her notebook with her wherever she went. Thoughts and ideas came into her head in the oddest of places, although she was finding that her creative imagination was lying somewhat dormant and she needed to wake it up. She sat in the evenings, after dinner, trying to create a new story, yet with some considerable difficulty. She was convinced her mind was clogged with stagnant energy that she had allowed to accumulate by fretting over the bad behaviour of others, directed at her. She decided to put down her pen until Sunday afternoon, when she would walk into town and sit in the fresh air. The town is always quiet on Sunday afternoons and there are plenty of benches placed in the pedestrian area.

The weather on Sunday was very pleasant, which pleased Marian. She did exactly as she had planned and walked into town.

Over the past few days she had become aware of her body and noticed how tense she had become. Her shoulders were lifted, her jaw tight. As she sat on her chosen bench she became mindful of her surroundings. Birds flew above, occasionally swooping down, optimistically looking for scraps. The shutters on shop fronts were closed, yet waiting to be opened next morning, to start the week all over again. She became aware of the stillness, the emptiness. Her bench felt hard and she could feel every dent, every gap in the wood. Her body was softening, her muscles melting. She felt she was becoming like her old lost self.

Marian closed her eyes and inhaled some deep breaths. As she did she felt the bench move beneath her, as if someone had sat down next to her. She opened her eyes to see no-one there. Yet at the same time she felt a presence. A pleasant smell of Jasmine wafted across her nostrils. It didn't faze her, in fact she felt serene and calm. The stagnant energy clogging her mind was becoming free like an unblocked drain. She knew at that moment, her creative imagination was returning. She walked home through the park, her head buzzing with new ideas for short stories.

Weather permitting Marian continued to make her weekly visits into town to sit on her bench. She was convinced she always felt a presence when she sat there, but wondered if it was her imagination working overtime. What she was sure of, is that, whenever she sat on her bench, her stories came easily and her pen flowed effortlessly. She packed her pen and precious notebook into her cotton shopping bag, as she did every week. She sat for a moment and observed in detail the buildings that lined the pedestrian street. The closest building to her had been, in its day, a beautiful Georgian home. The stylish front door was now sandwiched between two hideous shop fronts. Marian had a passion for old buildings, particularly from the Georgian and Victorian periods. Looking at the hideous shop fronts she thought how insensitive and disrespectful it was to architects of bygone days. *"What would they think if they could see their artwork now?"* she sadly thought. She looked up to the first floor window above the door. She saw something she had never noticed before: a blue plaque. Without hesitation, she shot up to see who had lived there. It was too high on the building to read, but fortunately there was an informative framed article at eye level.

This lovely house had once been the home of Charlotte Mary Brame, a writer of romantic novels. Marian gasped as a smile lit up her face. *Thank you Charlotte Mary Brame for joining me on my bench and thank you George Eliot for inspiring me with your wonderful quote.*

13

St. Anthony's Trilogy

The flight from New York to Dublin touched down on Irish tarmac at precisely 9.20am. All passengers have their own specific reasons for travelling to Ireland. There were three people on board who were catching a connecting flight to Kerry to complete their journey. The transition through customs went very smoothly, with no long wait at the luggage carousel. Some of the passengers had friends or relatives waiting to shower them with hugs and kisses. A few introduced themselves to the person holding their name on a placard and were escorted out of arrivals to a waiting car. Some were alone, making their way to the taxi rank.

The three passengers making a connecting flight to Kerry airport had a hour to wait. They welcomed the time, which allowed them to stretch their legs and take in a quick fix of coffee.

The hour passed quickly and once again they were touching down on Irish tarmac at Kerry airport. They made their way to the Hertz car rental office. All of them unaware they had made the long journey from New York to Kerry together. To add to their coincidences they were all driving to Kenmare, the gateway to the Ring of Kerry and all had reservations at the Lansdowne Hotel.

Leaving Kerry airport was a joy. There were no complicated road systems with a hundred and one road signs all competing for your attention. Just a simple two way N road.

Bob Carter was the first to leave the airport. Rushing was his normal New York pace of life, grabbing food on the hoof, hailing taxis and being somewhere half an hour ago. It was no surprise that he took the fast N22 route to Kenmare.

Two years ago Bob's bachelor Uncle Tom had passed away, leaving Bob his Kenmare home, that had been in the family for decades. Bob had given a lot of thought about what to do with the house. He wasn't a particularly sentimental man and had no desire to own a house in Ireland, despite loving to visit as a child. He did wrestle with the idea of putting it in the hands of Airbnb, but thought that might be too much of a hassle, with him living in America. Although it had been no hassle for him to organise a builder online and get the house refurbished. Bob wasn't completely devoid of sentimentality, so had decided to make the journey to Ireland, to revisit his childhood holiday memories and say a final goodbye to his

Uncle Tom's house. Never in his wildest dreams did he ever think that he would one day become the owner and subsequently the vendor. Uncle Tom was a big believer in St. Anthony, so Bob asked St. Anthony to find him a quick buyer.

Jane Horan left the airport with some trepidation. She had never driven on the left and furthermore, she had never been to Ireland. Two weeks after her Irish paternal grandparents married they emigrated from Ireland to New York. Jane was fascinated by her Irish roots and wanted to find out more about the Irish blood that ran free in her veins. She realised having a two week break in the town her grandparents left, was not sufficient to satisfy her longing to discover Ireland, or indeed herself.

Earlier in the year, in early spring, Jane was fortunate enough to come across a teaching post in Kenmare. She knew she must apply and she knew it was meant for her. Thanks to the wonder of technology she became the successful candidate. Everything had worked out perfectly, the timing couldn't have been better. She ended her teaching post in New York at Easter, which gave her the opportunity to visit Kenmare for two weeks in early summer. She hoped to secure a rental property ready for her return in autumn, when she would take up her teaching post at the local school.

Jane had researched the area for her drive to Kenmare. After navigating her way through Killarney, she took the N71 Molls Gap road. It guided her through spectacular and stunning scenery. It was early summer, ferns were lush and green as they miraculously grew out of rocks and carpeted ancient woodland. A break in the trees exposed a lake glinting in the sunshine. Purple rhododendrons complimented the many shades of green along the twisting mountainous road. The sign 'Ladies View' appeared at the roadside. Jane felt excitement. She had read about Ladies View. It was where Queen Victoria's ladies-in-waiting had stood to look down on the beauty and splendour of the Killarney lakes. She pulled into the allocated parking area and walked to the edge of the view. The silence was deafening. The mountains sat, secure and welcoming, like comfortable armchairs. The energy was immense. She knew then, there was nowhere else in the world she would want to be.

Joseph Clifford, the third passenger from New York and otherwise known simply as Joe, lived and worked in New York for the past 15 years. Joe is indeed a Kerry man by birth. His plan is to return to Kenmare in five years time. Joe Clifford liked to forward plan. He had come to Kenmare to buy a house, with a view to renting it out until his return in five years time, to reunite his heart and soul with his beloved Kenmare forever.

There was no other route Joe would contemplate other than the N71 Molls Gap route to Kenmare. Each twist in the road held a memory, like turning back the pages of a book to re-read the chapters of his life. The bike rides, the family picnics, the shopping trips to Killarney, they were all there, all enveloped in the arms of this stunning landscape.

Jane Horan was pulling out of the vantage point car park as Joe Clifford pulled in. To drive past Ladies View without stopping would be like a mortal sin to Joe. Happy tears of happy memories filled Joe's eyes. Leaving Ireland for New York had made big changes in Joe's life over the past 15 years. Apart from the natural ageing process from a fit athletic 25 year old to a less athletic 40 year old, Joe had exchanged his life of farming, fresh air and cows, for the diesel filled streets of New York. A somewhat stressful life in the city had given Joe the benefit of retiring at the comparatively young age of 45 and enough money in his bank account to purchase a house in Kenmare. Joe brought his thoughts back to the present; a surge of happiness filled his heart at the thought of house hunting tomorrow.

It was 8.30am and Jane Horan had just finished a delicious breakfast of perfectly scrambled eggs, smoked salmon, homemade brown soda bread and a tempting little pot of best butter. Jane neatly folded her napkin and made her way out of the breakfast room.

After an early morning walk on the pier Joe Clifford was ready for a full Irish, which would set him up for the day, before he began his house hunting journey. Joe entered the breakfast room five minutes after Jane had left and vacated his table 10 minutes before Bob Carter arrived.

Bob always took the opportunity for a lie in if circumstances permitted, and two weeks in relaxing Kenmare were exactly the right circumstances. After breakfast Bob consumed his second cup of hot strong coffee before taking a stroll down Main Street to the estate agents. They were selling Bob's house and holding the keys to his newly re-furbished property. Bob had put it on the market before he left New York. He had followed each step of the refurbishments online, but still wanted to see the completed project in the light of day. He also wanted to trace some of his boyhood memories and find the letters BC carved on a tree in the orchard.

Jane Horan spent her morning driving around the area. She wanted to live near the town for the convenience of being near to her job. Yet, on the other hand, wanted all the peace and privacy that nature offers, which in her eyes wasn't too much to ask. She had already paid a visit to St. Anthony and put in a request to find her the location she was looking for. She had driven a few routes out of Kenmare, but now decided to investigate the other side of the suspension bridge that crossed the beautiful Kenmare Bay. Soon after crossing the bridge there was a sign to the left saying Sheen Falls. She took the turn and immediately knew she had found her location. The trees arched across the road, the ferns were lush and large. She came to a beautiful stone bridge that crossed the Sheen Falls. It was hemmed either side with the loveliest of pink and white daisies all displaying their delicate beauty. Kenmare Bay ran alongside her to the left, mirroring the beauty of the sky. She took a right turn up into the hills, with each twist and turn confirming and without doubt, that she had found the townland where she wanted to live. As if out of nowhere a 'For Sale' sign appeared in the hedge. She slowed down to see a man unlocking the front door.

I bet he has bought that. She thought. *Lucky beggar.*

It was Bob Carter unlocking the door to his newly refurbished house. Pushing open the door, Bob stood motionless in the hallway. The decor had changed, but the energies remained. Bob, this not particularly sentimental man, had a lump in his throat and tears in his eyes. He was shocked how this tsunami wave of emotion washed over him and without warning. Childhood memories came flooding back to him. He could almost hear his Uncle Tom's voice greeting him. "Oh my God" he whispered, as he fumbled for his blue cotton handkerchief to dab his tears. He was having pangs of guilt to be selling Uncle Tom's house, but reconciled himself with the fact that he had restored a potentially derelict house and would be bringing life back to a little pocket of Ireland. The house was perfect and he was sure Uncle Tom would have loved it. He might have called it fancy, but he would have loved it. Bob made his way to the garden and into the orchard. He was searching for his initials that he had carved into a tree with the little penknife that Uncle Tom had given him for his twelfth birthday. Apple trees dominated the orchard, but in the far left corner there stood a beautiful beech tree. His initials had stood the test of time. He took his index finger and drew the letters BC over the carving. He felt he was touching his childhood.

At the same time Joe Clifford was walking into the estate agents at the bottom of Main Street. A voice bellowed out.

"Joe, Joe Clifford what in the name of God are you doing here. I thought you had emigrated to the Big Apple?"

Joe peered closer at the face that belonged to the voice.

"Oh my God. Ryan, Ryan Clancy. Jaysus it's good to see you. How long is it since we left school?"

Joe and Ryan exchanged the longest, firmest handshake, followed by a reassuring pat on the back. After they were both over the shock of reuniting, Joe told Ryan his plans of buying a house to rent for five years before returning to Kenmare for good.

"Joe it's your lucky day. Someone is watching over you. I think I have the very thing. It's recently come on the market and it's completely refurbished, perfect for rental so it is. The fella that is selling doesn't want complicated chains holding up completion. If you like the house, I'd say your cash purchase would be the very thing he's looking for.

It's in a lovely wee spot. About five kilometres out of town."

"My God Ryan that sounds grand. I can't wait to see it."

"I can run you out this evening. The quicker you see it, the better. I know it won't be long on the market. Meet me here at five o'clock. We'll go and view it and then you can buy me a pint for old times' sake."

Joe held his hand out to Ryan.

"That's a deal Ryan. Holy Mother of God, I still can't believe us meeting after all these years."

Ryan smiled. "I'll see ye at five o'clock."

Jane Horan had explored what seemed, every lane, nook and cranny around Kenmare. Although she had found her perfect location, she was sensible and realistic enough to know she would have to compromise and settle for whatever she could get. After all she was only looking to rent. She had heard residential rental properties were scarce in Kenmare.

My day is done, she thought. *I will go back to the hotel and have a luxury afternoon bath. Tomorrow I will hit the estate agents.*

At five o'clock prompt Joe Clifford arrived at the estate agents. He had popped into the church earlier to ask St. Anthony to find him his forever home in Kenmare. Ryan was ready and waiting. He picked up his car keys, together with the house details file and escorted Joe to his car.

"That's a grand car you have there Ryan. You must be doing alright."

"Oh not so bad Joe. We did have some lean years, but thanks be to God things started to fatten up."

Ryan pulled into the driveway of Bob Carter's house. Joe went quiet.

"Are you ok Joe? You seem to have gone quiet."

"I am blown away Ryan. I haven't been inside yet and I am in awe of the place. This wee site has such a special feeling."

"It does indeed Joe. I knew you wouldn't fail to like it."

"Like it is an understatement Ryan. Let's go inside to see if it continues to please."

The house was everything and more. Joe couldn't stress enough to Ryan how much he wanted it.

"Ryan tell the vendor I will pay him the full asking price on condition he takes it off the market."

Ryan looked at his watch.

"It's only six thirty. I'll give him a call now and then we'll go for that pint."

Joe gave Ryan the thumbs up. "Perfect, Ryan, perfect."

After several rings Bob Carter answered his phone.

"Bob, it's Ryan. I have a serious purchaser for your house. No chain and a cash buyer. Full asking price on condition you take it off the market."

"Snap his hand off Ryan. Snap his hand off. Tell him I am delighted with that deal."

"I will so Bob, I will so."

Ryan ended the call. Joe was staring at him, eagerly waiting in anticipation. Ryan went silent and looked glum.

"Well, what did he say?"

Ryan continued to look glum.

"Well, I'm afraid he said, I've to snap your hand off. I've to snap your hand off, so I have."

"Jaysus you had me going there, you gobshite."

The two men laughed while offering a high five in unison.

"Come on Joe, I think that's two pints you owe me."

"Ryan you can have champagne, so you can. I am absolutely over the moon. I never thought finding a house in Kenmare would be so easy."

The day was closing. The pale moon was rising over Kenmare Bay bringing with it a sense of tranquillity and reassurance that tomorrow would be a good day.

The gentle sunrise warmed the streets and Jane Horan was having an earlier shower than usual. To-day was the day she was hoping and praying to secure a property to rent, but she wanted to pay another visit to St. Anthony, before searching the estate agents, just in case he hadn't heard her the first time she asked.

Jane nervously pushed open the door of the estate agents office. The sales assistant looked up from her computer. She smiled.

"Hello, how you doing. It's a lovely day, is it not?"

Jane smiled back. She noticed her name badge read 'Siobhan.' She had to hold back from telling Siobhan she had lipstick on her teeth.

"Hello. I'm enquiring about houses for long term rent."

Jane proceeded to tell Siobhan the saga of moving from America and of her plans to move to Kenmare in the autumn. Ryan was eavesdropping in the background. He stepped forward.

"Sorry to interrupt Siobhan, but how long are you looking to rent?"

"Oh about four to five years, if that's possible. I will be renting out my apartment back home. Just as a safety net you know, in case I don't settle here, but I am sure I will."

Ryan was flabbergasted. It went through his mind that this was the very tenant Joe was looking for. He was convinced there was some divine intervention going on somewhere.

"Siobhan I'll take over, we have a new rental on the books. Only came on last night."

Before Jane could come to terms with her luck, she was being whisked away by Ryan to view her potential new home. She was intrigued, nervous and excited as Ryan drove up Main Street, turning right at the Lansdowne Hotel and passing the little book shop on the left. She couldn't wait to visit this lovely wee shop and treat herself to a new book for her journey back to New York. At the end of Shelbourne Street Ryan turned left, the very same direction she had driven yesterday. Ryan was explaining how Joe was in the process of buying and then wanting to rent for five years. Jane couldn't take in his words, they were scrambled in her head. The only thing that held her concentration was the route Ryan was taking. As the car passed over the suspension bridge, Kenmare Bay sat in all its splendour. It was calm and tranquil reflecting the beauty of the day. Jane caught a glimpse of a hungry heron optimistically fishing off the edge of a rock.

How could my grandparents leave such a beautiful place? she asked herself.

"You seem desperately quiet Jane. You're not having second thoughts are you?"

"Oh no Ryan. I can one hundred percent assure you I am not."

Jane then realised Ryan was taking the exact same route as she had driven yesterday. They drove over the same little stone bridge. She wanted to wave at the pink and white daisies and say "Hello I'm back."

"Not long to go Jane, we are nearly there. Always seems further than it is, when you don't know where you are going."

Jane smiled. "Yes I suppose it does."

They were approaching the 'For Sale' sign that Jane saw yesterday, only this time it had a 'Sale Agreed' sign on it. She remembered thinking how lovely the house and grounds looked. Ryan slowed down; his left indicator was clicking away as he turned into the driveway.

"But this house has been sold." Jane said curiously.

"I know. This is what I was telling you back there. The new owner wants to rent it out for five years, until he comes back to Kenmare permanently."

"Oh yes, I remember now."

Well I will tell him I remember, even if my thoughts were elsewhere, she thought.

Ryan showed Jane around the house and grounds. She was fit to burst with happiness. It was everything she had hoped for and more. Ryan could sense her excitement.

"I take it you like it Jane?"

"Ryan, it is perfect. I can't believe my luck. I would love to secure the tenancy as soon as we get back to the office."

"Well I'll have to get the contract drawn up and run it past Joe. Pop into the office after mid-day tomorrow and I'll have the tenancy agreement ready for you to sign."

"Ryan that's awesome. I can't wait."

Ryan drove Jane back into Kenmare before ringing Joe to tell him the good news.

"Hi Joe, I have found you your dream tenant for the next five years. She is coming into the office after mid-day tomorrow to sign the agreement.

Could you pop in tomorrow around 10am to make sure you are happy with it?"

"Ryan you are a star. I will be there promptly at 10am."

"I have to tell you Joe I have never in all my days made a sale, a purchase and a tenancy all on the one property and in such a short time. It's unheard of. I think someone up there is looking down on all three of ye. I know we have all the legal stuff to go through, but I am sure it will all go through without a hitch."

The surprising thing is Ryan had never told Bob his buyer was from America, nor had he mentioned to Joe his tenant was from America. With the whirlwind of transactions over the past week or so, it must have slipped his mind.

In a few days time Bob, Joe and Jane would be making their way back to the States. It's no surprise to know they were all booked on the same flight back to New York. Like ships that pass in the night, they were all oblivious to their connection.

Bob Carter had slowed down and melted into the Irish pace of life, he looked younger too. He was delighted with his house sale and so happy he revisited his childhood memories. In his heart of hearts, he knew New York was his home.

Joe Clifford was sad to be leaving Kenmare, but content in the knowledge he would be returning to his forever happy place in the near future.

Jane Horan was just bursting with happiness and contentment. Coming to Kenmare made her understand herself. She knew she had found her true roots and what's more she felt connected.

14

Early Morning Flight

Her flight from Madrid to Birmingham took off at 7.30am. The Captain announced himself, but she didn't catch his name.

Despite it being an early morning flight, it was a beautiful day to take to the skies and look down in sheer wonderment on planet Earth. Blue clear skies make even the most nervous of passengers feel a lot calmer. That certainly applied to Helen Clarke. She loved a window seat with a clear view.

They were about half way into the flight when Helen became aware that the Captain had not given out any information. Not even the name of the group of islands they had recently flown over. Apart from wanting to know the weather forecast in Birmingham, it reassured her to hear the Captain's voice. In Helen's mind, if the Captain was communicating with the passengers, then all was well in the cockpit. Her nervousness got the better of her. She alerted the stewardess.

"Excuse me, but the Captain hasn't been talking to us. I would have liked to have known the name of the group of islands a little way back. Makes me nervous when I don't hear from him." She gave a little embarrassed laugh.

"I will go and ask the Captain and let you know."

The stewardess returned within five minutes. She leaned over to Helen and whispered, "the Captain has invited you to the cockpit."

Helen's eyes nearly popped out of her head. "Oh Lord," she muttered.

Helen followed the stewardess to the cockpit and tentatively entered.

"I am sorry to be a nuisance," she said coyly.

"That's ok. Angie explained that you are a nervous passenger. I can assure you everything is fine. I thought most people would be a little sleepy and would want some quiet time."

He laughed as he turned to look at Helen full face. Helen thought he stared at her a little too long, making her feel uncomfortable. She awkwardly thanked him and returned to her seat feeling quite excited and reassured. She had never been in the cockpit before.

Helen was divorced. She and her husband Peter had so desperately wanted children. Sadly,

Helen's infertility and failed IVF treatments put an enormous strain on their relationship. Helen would have been happy to adopt, but Peter was totally against it. He wanted his own children, or nothing.

After spending six years of living and teaching in Spain, Helen was returning to England to have a period of rest and a re-evaluation of her life. She believed everything happened for a reason and was quite confident that shutting the door on her life in Spain would allow another door to open in England. Anticipating her unknown new life filled her with excitement, yet lurking behind the excitement, trepidation was also adding to her mix of emotions. She had rented out her English house, together with the use of her precious mini to Kay, a very dear college friend. Kay had been working in Birmingham for the past six years, but had moved back to London just one month ago. Their career timing couldn't have worked out better and Helen couldn't have asked for a better tenant.

Ding dong. "Please remain seated and fasten your seat belts. We are beginning our descent into Birmingham. The weather is sunny with a chill in the air temperature."

As the stewardess was making final checks up and down the plane, she stopped at Helen and told her the Captain would like to see her again after they had landed. "He has some more information for you."

Helen was mystified. She waited until most of the other passengers had disembarked. Once again she nervously entered the cockpit.

"Hello again. You asked to see me?"

"Yes Helen. I did."

"How do you know my name?"

"Helen you don't remember me do you? I'm John Hughes. We were in sixth form together. I remembered you straight away. I couldn't talk to you for long earlier. Here's my number, give me a ring; it would be lovely to catch up and reminisce. Sorry to be abrupt, but you will have to leave the plane now."

Helen was taken aback as she peered more closely.

"Yes, Yes. I do remember you. I just didn't recognise you. Thank you. Yes ok."

She walked down the steps of the aircraft, her mind in a whirl and her day had only just started.

Helen's small end of terraced house was about 30 minutes journey from the airport. She couldn't wait to get home and digest all the food for thought that she had been served on the flight.

After an afternoon siesta, Helen's mind was a lot clearer. Trepidation had left her thoughts and excitement was definitely her dominant emotion. Her main priority was to raid the supermarket and fill her fridge with healthy nourishing food. A Chinese take-a-way, although very tempting, was not her idea of a healthy meal.

With the back seat of her Mini Cooper laden with over-filled carrier bags, a bunch of fresh flowers and a bottle of wine, she set off back to her little house, to make it look like a home. Although Kay had treated it like it was her own.

A week had passed by quite quickly. It was Sunday and the coat Helen had arrived in from Spain was still draped over the banister. She tried to iron out the creases, firmly stroking the fabric. She heard the sound of crumpled paper in the pocket. Lifting it out, she realised it was the phone number of John Hughes.

I'll have to think about that, she pondered.

She pinned his note on her message board. Helen didn't feel physically attracted to John, but for old times' sake she would like to contact him. It would be good to find out what has happened in his world and get all nostalgic about their school days.

After indulging in a full English she declared it was going to be a pyjama day.

Right! She thought. *I have got to either ring this number, or throw it away.*

Helen pressed the numbers of the key pad. It rang several times. The answer machine kicked in.

"Hello this is John. Please leave your name and number with a brief message and I will get back to you."

"Message, what message?" She cried. She hadn't prepared herself to leave a message.

She stammered and stuttered and eventually left a garbled message along with her number, which was just about decipherable.

A week had passed by when John finally returned Helen's call.

"Helen, hello. Sorry I didn't get back to you before. I've had such a frantic week."

John and Helen arranged to go for lunch on Wednesday. They both found each other's company very pleasant and relaxing. They laughed, talked and never had awkward silences. Lunch was such a success they decided to make it a regular occurrence.

Their friendship blossomed. Helen couldn't have asked for a more beautiful relationship. John made her feel special and treated her with such care and consideration. Helen had told John that she was divorced, single and wanted to stay that way.

John never divulged his romantic status, until one day, he asked Helen if he could confide in her. Helen was flattered that John felt he had her trust. John explained that he was a widower and a single parent.

"I am so sorry John. How do you manage for child care?"

"Well that's one of my problems. My mum looks after Zak, my son, when I am working, but I know it is getting too much for her. Especially when I am on a long haul flight. However, my big secret that I want to share with you, is that I am gay. I have never told anyone before. I always knew I was gay, but couldn't come to terms with it. If I couldn't, how could I expect my parents to? I did all the conventional things like getting married and having a child. Now I am widowed I want to remain single. I never want to feel the pressure of getting married again, or to announce that I am gay. I never want Zak to know."

Helen tried to reassure John that it was ok to 'come out'. John was adamant he was happy with his life as it is.

That evening Helen couldn't think of anything else other than John's situation. Their friendship had become so special that she felt very protective and caring towards him.

Their next meeting was in three weeks time and Helen had invited John and his son Zak for Sunday lunch. It was so apparent how John idolised Zak. He was his life, his everything. Helen's eyes filled with tears when she saw the love between them.

After a lovely home cooked lunch and a walk in the park to feed the ducks, Zak's little body couldn't fight the sleep. His little head dropped onto Helen's shoulder. Her heart melted. She felt so much affection towards him. John gently lifted him and took him to sleep on the day bed in the back room. Zak looked so small in John's arms.

Helen made coffee and she and John sat side by side on the sofa. For the first time there was an awkward silence between them. John was the first to break it.

"Helen, does it make any difference to our friendship that I am gay?"

"No John, not at all. In fact I feel privileged that you felt you could confide in me."

"Thank you Helen, that means so much to me."

"I have been giving your situation with Zak and his child care a lot of thought. How would you feel if I became his live in nanny and housekeeeper? I do need to work you know. I don't want to marry again and I can't have children. I do know I have enough love in me to love Zak as if he were my own. I have also grown to love you John in a very special way."

The silence returned. Helen turned to look at John. There were tears rolling down his cheeks.

"John, what's wrong? I didn't mean to upset you."

"No you haven't. My tears are tears of happiness and relief. You are such a wonderful person and I love you too in that very special way. I would love nothing more than for you to live with us and make us into a little family."

Helen's longing for a child had been fulfilled and John was happy to be seen as living a conventional life. They had both found happiness and contentment in the safety and security of their very special friendship.

15

The Last Piece of The Jigsaw

"Bye Olivia. I shouldn't be too late. I'm only playing nine holes today."

Olivia was balancing on a stepladder washing the picture rails that adorned the beautiful Victorian hallway.

"Bye Owen. Would you pick up some milk on your way back?"

That was fifteen years ago and the last time Olivia saw her husband. All the usual procedures were carried out. Police investigations were made. Hospital patient lists were checked. Every inch of the golf course was searched. When all avenues of investigation had been exhausted, Owen Metcalfe was put on the missing persons list.

Olivia Metcalfe had spent fifteen years living in hope, fifteen years of visiting pubs Owen had frequented and places that were special to them. She scoured the streets of nearby towns trying to get glimpses of the faces lying in shop doorways. The face she was looking for was that of Owen fifteen years ago. She tried to imagine how he would look now.

Would he be fatter, maybe thinner? Would he be lined? Maybe his hair is grey. Or maybe he could have retained his dark curly locks. Maybe he has lost all his hair.

All these 'maybes' tormented Olivia and deprived her of sleep well into the dark hours.

She loved him so much; they loved each other so much. She often went over the good times they shared. She remembered the excitement she felt the day they went to choose their wedding rings. They had two circles interlinked with the date of their wedding engraved inside each ring. Owen said it represented them, two circles that couldn't be broken, two circles that also stood for Olivia and Owen. She touched her ring and turned it round and round her finger.

"Where are you Owen, where are you?" She said out loud.

Olivia used to play golf with Owen at their local golf course, although she certainly wasn't up to his standard. She hadn't picked up her golf clubs since Owen had gone missing. The thought of playing again would evoke happy memories, yet paradoxically be too painful.

Olivia's lifelong friend Wendy, also a golfer, had an idea that might get Olivia back on the golf course. Wendy suggested to Olivia that they went to play just nine holes on a course that wasn't local, somewhere she hadn't played with Owen. Olivia was quite aware she was becoming a hermit and knew it made perfect sense to put some life back into her life. She phoned Wendy the next day and told her she was willing to give it a go. Wendy arranged everything. She decided they would make a weekend of it. She booked a delightful little guest house near to a golf course. It was about a hundred miles away on the coast. They arrived on a Thursday afternoon, checked into the guest house, unpacked and then went for a bracing walk on the beach before dinner in the evening.

"Gosh Wendy I am feeling so much better just being here. Never mind the fresh sea air in my lungs."

"I am so pleased Olivia. I have been worried about you. You've not had a holiday since... well for a long time."

Olivia stood on the first tee taking deep breaths, swinging her arms across her chest and slapping her back. There was a nip in the air on the early morning golf course, but that was compensated by the amber glow that filled the sky and the atmospheric mist that rolled in off the sea.

"Are you ok Olivia?"

"Yes I'm ok, but I'd be lying if I said I wasn't thinking about Owen."

"Of course you are and that's quite natural and understandable. Now, put your best foot forward and don't look backwards."

After all the years off the golf course Olivia was surprised at how well she was playing. She shed a little tear as she remembered Owen saying, "I'll race you to the flag." For some reason he always liked to take the flag out of the hole. She could see him in her mind's eye, like a little boy. Her tears turned into smiles. Owen could always make her smile.

"Wendy I am so grateful you persuaded me to take this break. It really has been so therapeutic. I almost feel I am beginning to start a new life. I'll never forget your kindness."

"That's what friends are for Olivia, that's what friends are for."

They had finally reached the ninth hole. Wendy removed the flag for Olivia.

"Come on Olivia this is quite a long putt, let's see if you can down it from there."

Olivia was taking her game seriously. She lined herself up, checked her stance and putted her ball. It took a straight line, started to go wide, and then miraculously curved towards the hole as if it was being magnetically steered.

"Yes, yes, yes I did it!" Olivia screamed. She ran excitedly towards the hole to retrieve her ball. As she picked it up she also picked up a small hard object. "Oh what's this?" She wiped away a little bit of mud and grass clippings, to uncover a gold wedding ring. Taking a tissue from her pocket she gave the ring a good polish.

"How sad, someone has lost their wedding ring. OH MY GOD, I don't believe it, I think it's Owen's."

"What do you mean Owen's?"

"It's the engravings inside. It has the two circles and the date of our wedding." replied Olivia.

She promptly slid her ring from her finger.

"Look Wendy, look at the engraving in my ring and then look at this one. They are identical."

"Holy shit! You are right. What are you going to do?"

"Nothing Wendy, not yet anyway. I really need to give this some thought."

Needless to say the night was long for Olivia. She tossed and turned until the dawn chorus.

The two women were sharing a twin bedded room, so Olivia was careful not to make a sound. She slipped into her tracksuit bottoms and hooded fleece, grabbed her sunglasses and tiptoed out of the room. She needed to take a brisk walk on the beach to clear her head.

The town was just waking up. The odd shutter was being raised disturbing the peace of the early morning. Pigeons swooped down scavenging any tiny morsel left by Friday night revellers. The air was crisp and cool, but at the same time the early sunrise was bright and warming the streets. A bus stopped, picking up a couple of early shift workers.

Olivia turned off into a side street that led to the beach. The temperature dropped noticeably. She pulled her hoody over her head to protect her from the cool breeze coming in from the sea. The rows of terraced houses looked darker, as the sunlight would be visiting them later. Lights were being switched on and the occasional car had its ignition started, exhaling fumes from its dormant lungs. The monotonous whir and rattling of milk crates could be heard from a distant milk float. This made Olivia smile.

Owen used to say to her, "When I grow up I'm going to be a milkman with my own float."

They would fall about laughing. The whirring had stopped, but had been replaced by the non-melodic whistle of the milkman.

Strange, she thought. *I can hear him, but I can't actually see him.*

Then before she knew it BANG. He had appeared from behind a hedge and through the gateway of one of the small terraced house gardens and bumped into her. It was a wonder her sunglasses remained on her face.

"Oh I'm sorry love. No damage done." he said, as he gave her a reassuring squeeze on the arm.

He continued across the street, resuming his tuneless whistle.

His voice echoed in her head. She turned sharply to look at him, while pulling her hoody even further over her head, until it was practically covering her face.

It's him, it's Owen. No damage done, no damage done! What about the last fifteen bloody years? her voice screamed in her head.

The blood drained from her body and her face turned ashen. Despite her jelly legs she managed to continue to the beach.

Finding the nearest bench she collapsed in utter shock. She had often wondered what she would do and feel in this situation. Now she knew and it wasn't what she expected. It was like finding that last piece of the jigsaw. When the missing piece is found it completes the picture. It can be put back in its box and forgotten about. After Olivia's initial shock that is exactly how she was feeling. Her picture had been completed. All her 'maybes' had been resolved and boxed away. A considerable weight had been lifted.

Surprisingly, the love and respect she had for Owen for all those years disappeared. As for his wedding ring, Olivia found great delight in throwing it into the ocean.

16

The Kerry Connection

It was the morning Martha Brown had been dreading. She opened her eyes and knew something major was happening that day, but wasn't focused enough to bring it to mind. Then she remembered. Adrenaline surged into her stomach and flooded into her chest before making its way up into her neck and down her arms. Her body had been attacked with anxiety.

"Breathe," she told herself. "Just breathe. This time tomorrow it will all be over."

Martha's husband appeared in the bedroom doorway.

"Are you ok my love? It's your big day today and I've brought you a nice wee cup of tea."

"George, I can't drink it, I'm nil by mouth. Remember?"

"Oh Jesus Martha I completely forgot. I'll take it out of temptations way. You had better be after getting yourself up. I have to get you to hospital by 7.30am."

Martha swung her legs over the side of the bed and planted her feet firmly on the ground. She placed her hands over her left knee and gently massaged the swollen, painful deformity. Despite the agonising pain she was sorry to be saying goodbye to the knee that had carried and supported her for almost sixty five years. Martha prayed to the Lord to keep her safe and asked for an angel to guide the surgeon's hand.

"Come on Martha. You can open your eyes now. You are all done."

She could feel a gentle hand stroking the side of her cheek.

"Is it all over nurse?"

"Yes Martha, it's all over and you are doing fine."

Martha's bed was wheeled down the corridor before turning into Ward C to occupy the waiting vacant space that sandwiched her between Christina on her left and Mary on her right. With Martha's earlier encounter with nervous exhaustion and the administered drugs taking control, she was in no fit state to exchange pleasantries with her fellow 'inmates'.

As the afternoon sunlight flooded the ward, Martha was beginning to stir and become more aware of her surroundings, even managing to exchange smiles with other patients. Her thoughts went to the holiday she was taking in autumn to her beautiful Irish home. Martha and George were both Irish, but had moved to England many years ago. England had offered them good opportunities, for which they were truly grateful, but their hearts lay in their beloved homeland.

Martha was beginning to feel a little hungry and welcomed the rattling of the tea time trolley. She had introduced herself to Mary and Christina and considering the trauma they had all been through, the banter between them was good. It lifted their spirits and pleasantly passed the time. Martha had a good night's sleep and thanked the Lord for her morning cuppa.

No nil by mouth this morning and she was determined it would be no nil by make-up either. It felt like it was going to be an effort, but Martha always took her bag of tricks out every morning and carefully applied her make-up, even if she was staying at home for the day. It made her feel better and feeling better was exactly what she wanted. After breakfast and the morning rituals on the ward, Martha and Mary were placed side by side in their chairs at the side of the beds, with their operated legs elevated. They chatted away very easily, so much so that they seemed like lifelong friends.

"Are you going on holiday this year Martha?"

"Yes we are hoping to go in autumn, God willing."

"Oh that's lovely. We should be well healed by then Martha. Have you decided where you are going?"

"Yes Mary, we are off to Ireland."

"Ireland? We have a house over there in Kerry."

"Get away, are you serious? We have a house in Kerry too."

"Oh my God!" the women exclaimed in unison.

The touch paper had been lit. They were off like rockets. And when they found out they both lived on the edge of the same town, there was no stopping them. They went through the town with a fine tooth comb. From the moods of Mrs. Doyle in the post office, to which was the best butcher.

"Do you know Mary I haven't laughed so much in a long time. I have to confess I am quite enjoying my stay in hospital."

"Well you know what they say Martha, laughter is the best medicine."

On the day they left hospital Martha and Mary exchanged phone numbers. They phoned each other every week to compare notes on their progress, and their friendship blossomed.

Autumn had arrived and God had willed that Martha spend it in her Irish home in her beloved Kerry. She was so grateful to the Lord and her surgeon for enabling her to walk on the beach without pain. Martha had established her own little tradition during the first week of her arrival in Kerry. It was that she laid flowers on the grave of her ancestors on her father's side. Although Martha hadn't known most of these ancestors, they were important to her and laying flowers for them, was like connecting with them. She bought the flowers late on Friday afternoon and decided she would visit the graveyard early Saturday morning. It was a crisp beautiful autumn morning with a low atmospheric mist encircling the mountains. Yet it was apparent the sun was going to take over in an hour or two.

Martha parked her car in the lane at the side of the graveyard. She opened the little gate that squeaked, just like it squeaked twenty years ago. There were mainly Celtic cross gravestones in various sizes, but in the distance was one very large Celtic cross, which looked down on Martha's great grandfather and other ancestors. Martha could see a small female figure standing under the cross. She could see the crisp cool air of the stranger's breath leave her mouth. The closer she got to the graveside Martha couldn't believe her eyes.

"God Almighty Mary, what in the name of Jesus are you doing here? How lovely to see you."

"Oh Martha how lovely to see you too. How's the knee?"

"Oh it's grand and yourself? How long have you been in Kerry Mary?"

"We got a last minute flight. Just needed to get away Martha. I can't believe us bumping into each other like this."

"I have come to put these flowers on my great grandfather's grave".

Martha respectfully laid the flowers at the foot of the cross and blessed herself.

"Did you say your great grandfather?"

"Yes Mary I did."

"But Martha he is my great grandfather."

The two women nearly exploded. They could not believe, for all the Guinness in Ireland, that they had this connection.

"Come on Mary we need a drink and I am not talking about coffee. I think we have a lot to talk about."

It transpired that Martha and Mary's grandfathers were brothers and their great grandfather was the same man. Mary's grandparents left Ireland and went to live in America when Mary's father, Joseph, was five years old. As a young man Joseph left America and went to live in England. He met a girl in Coventry whose parents came from County Cork. They had two children Mary and Michael. Despite being born in England Mary felt every bit as Irish as the shamrock.

"Would you believe Mary what was going to unfold the day we had our knees replaced?"

"What is meant to be Martha, what is meant to be. Everything happens for a reason as they say."

"Yes Mary and I can't tell you enough that the reason has made me very happy."

"Me too Martha, me too."

17

Kindness

Kindness is a beautiful act that can soothe sorrows, melt away pain, or quite simply lift the clouds on a rainy day. Listening acts of kindness are free, yet priceless to the person receiving. Perception is the key and kindness opens the door, so even a stranger can walk through and pour out their heart, which allows you to provide that listening ear, in silence, without judgement. Your time to listen is free, yet at the same time priceless, as time is the most precious thing we have.

You will see strain lift from their face, weight fall from their shoulders. Back inside their door, their worries are easier and calmness descends.

The kindness of giving is a magical act. Giving food to the homeless not only feeds their bellies, it feeds their souls. Makes them feel worthy, like they matter, because someone cares. To give an arm round a shoulder or a gentle squeeze of the hand, brings comfort and hope.

Actions of kindness certainly do speak louder than words.

18

Laburnum House

Laburnum House is a large detached Victorian dwelling sitting majestically at the end of Blackberry Lane, in the heart of the Warwickshire countryside. It has been occupied by several families over the years. Some bringing sorrow, some bringing shame, some departing from this world within its walls, whilst others took their first breath. For the past 30 years, or a little more, it has witnessed much love, laughter and happiness.

Charles Graham and his wife Elizabeth moved into the house in 1950 just after they were married. They went on to have four children, two sons, Peter and Robert, and two daughters, Susan and Janet.

Charles Graham was a retired banker, he had a happy marriage and his children grew up to be successful well balanced young adults. They were perceived in the village as the perfect family.

Janet and Susan both became teachers. Susan was teaching in London and Janet was teaching at the same primary school in the village which she had attended. She was still living with her parents while she was saving for a deposit to buy her own home. Peter had gone a little further afield and was a partner in a civil engineering company in Edinburgh. Robert was the less academic of his siblings. He had a love of nature and the thought of working indoors, from nine to five, was too much for him to bear. He trained as a landscape gardener and, with his creative and imaginative talent, he became very much in demand. He still lived at home, but was in the process of refurbishing a house a few miles from his parents.

It was half term break. Elizabeth and Janet set off early on the Saturday morning to visit Susan in London. Elizabeth loved to spend time with her two daughters. It was becoming rare to see them both together. She still loved to buy them a little treat, just as she did when they were little girls. Robert was taking advantage of the good weather and spending the weekend working at his house. The house was almost complete, apart from fitting kitchen cupboards and other finishing touches. The weather was being very kind, so Robert thought he would take advantage of that, and work in the garden. After all it was his favourite place to be. As a landscape gardener he had all the tools, knowledge and equipment to carry out work on his own garden. He had incorporated a small pond in his garden design, and thought it was the perfect day to dig out the pit in preparation.

Charles was having a relaxing time at home reading and pottering in his greenhouse.

Elizabeth and Janet wouldn't be home until Monday afternoon, so Robert had promised his father he would take him out for an early bird meal at their local. Robert returned home about four o'clock so he could have a well earned soak in the bath.

"Hi Dad. I'm back. Just going to have a soak in the bath. Are you hungry?"

Robert got not as much as an "ok" as a reply. He then became aware the house had a very loud silence. There were four reception rooms downstairs, a large drawing room, a dining room, a library and a small room which they called the snug. He looked in all the rooms leaving the library until last. The beautiful mahogany desk and captain's chair were over by the large sash windows. As Robert opened the door he saw his father slumped over the desk.

"Dad wake up, we are going out for dinner, remember?"

There wasn't a murmur, not a movement, not a breath. As Robert got nearer to his father, he could see an empty bottle of tablets. He felt his father's pulse. There was nothing. The blood drained from Robert's body. His face turned ashen. He was numb. He was in shock. His head went into panic mode.

"What do I do? Who do I ring? The police, the ambulance, the doctor?"

The telephone in the hallway rang. Robert was startled. He was now in a dilemma as to whether to answer it or not.

"Oh my God it might be Mum. Better answer it, or she will worry."

As he reached for the receiver he saw an envelope obscuring the dial. He had to think fast.

"If it's Mum how can I tell her? I can't."

"Hello. Oh hello Mum. Yes I'm fine. Just a bit out of breath, I have just run down the stairs to answer the phone. Dad's gone out for a walk. Yes I'm sure, I'm fine. You enjoy the rest of your weekend. Say "hello" to Susan for me. Must dash, I am just running a bath. See you Monday. Byee. Bye."

Robert stared at the envelope. He picked it up with sweaty, shaking hands. 'Elizabeth' was written neatly on the front. It didn't look like the hand of a man contemplating suicide. The envelope wasn't sealed. He lifted the flap and pulled out a single sheet of blue writing paper. The words were dancing around the page. His state of panic was making it hard to focus, tears were now blurring his vision and his heart thumping hard in his chest. He took a deep breath and somehow found his composure.

The letter read:

My Dear Elizabeth,

I am so deeply sorry to leave you this way. I have been living a pretence for many years. Now I am retired and in the departure lounge phase of my life, I realise I can't continue to have the best of both worlds anymore.

I have been sharing my life between you and another woman, Fiona. I can't live with myself anymore. I can't live with the shame, or the guilt. Life is one big struggle and is now too heavy for me to bear.

I hope your days remain happy for as long as you live. If you can find it in your heart, I hope my darling, you will forgive me.

Tell the children I love them and believe me when I say, I have always loved you.

Forever Yours

Charles

Fiona! Who the bloody hell is Fiona? I can't let Mum know all this, the suicide, the affair, the cheating and the lies, it would kill her. She is devoted to him. I have to think and I have to think fast.

Fortunately Robert hadn't actually booked a table at The Red Lion, as he knew they would always find a space for him and his dad. It was a relief for him not to have to make a cancellation.

Robert went and backed his van under the car port and outside of the kitchen door. He rolled a tarpaulin over the beautiful Persian carpet that adorned the library floor. He stood motionless as he glimpsed childhood memories. Memories of a wet Sunday afternoon next to the fire, with his brother and sisters sitting at their father's feet on the same beautiful carpet, listening to instalments of *'Wind in The Willows'*. He remembered how beautifully it was read. He wished that what he was about to do was a bad dream.

Robert struggled to lift his father's body down onto the floor. He felt sick and couldn't believe where he found the strength to drag Charles into his van. His emotional state, together with the shock and lack of food, should have extracted all the strength from his tired muscles. He now had a plan in his mind. He would take Charles and place him in the pit he had dug out for his pond, fill it with concrete and make it into a hard standing area. He would ring the police on Sunday night saying that he thought his dad was out on a walk, but hadn't returned home yet. He would tell them that it was unlike his dad to walk in the dark. His thoughts were now racing. Panic was taking over. Never ever in his life did he think that one day he would be trying to dispose of his father's body. His thoughts were becoming entangled. All wrapped together like a messed up ball of knitting wool.

Hang on. What would Dad be wearing if he was on a walk? Of course he never goes anywhere without his cap.

He grabbed his dad's cap and coat off the hallstand. He also took a walking pole to make it look more genuine. He was astounded how his mind was now thinking.

Robert's house was very secluded, he arrived there around 9pm. He opened his front door and almost collapsed into the hallway.

"What am I doing?" he asked himself.

He felt like he had committed murder, but knew he had to protect his mother. It was going to be enough of a shock and upset for her, without learning she had been living with a cheat and a liar. Despite all of that, she would still be devastated by Charles's suicide. Needless to say, Robert hardly slept that night.

He was up early carrying out the gruesome task of burying his father's body.

"Oh Dad, why oh why?" he kept repeating.

He said a prayer over what had become Charles's grave. Robert felt sick, he felt ill, he felt disloyal for not letting his father have a proper funeral, but he didn't think he had a choice in the matter. He felt there was no alternative as far as his mother was concerned.

He returned back to his father's house around 5pm. Robert had it very clear in his head what he would do. At 6pm he would ring The Red Lion to enquire if his father was there. He thought that might convince the police he was looking for his father. At 6.45pm he would ring the police. He had hoovered the study to make sure there were no drag marks in the carpet. The empty bottle of tablets and the suicide note had both been buried with Charles. Robert was doing all he could to protect his mum from the truth. He phoned the police as planned. It was a small village and everyone knew Charles. The police officer said he wasn't overly concerned at this stage.

"If we went out looking for everyone who stayed out late, we'd never get anything done. I should wait til tomorrow. He's probably gone in for a cup of tea somewhere."

Robert was convincing himself that Charles had gone missing.

I will wait and tell Mum and Janet tomorrow, before I ring the police again.

He found it reassuring to talk to himself and tell himself of every intention he had in his head.

He heard Janet's car on the drive.

Oh hell, I hope I can hold myself together. Come on Robert you have to.

He heard the key in the lock, the hall door opened.

"Hello darling, we are home."

Robert walked out of the kitchen.

"Hello Mum, Janet."

"You look tired Robert. Are you ok? I expect you have been over doing it on your refurbishment. You really shouldn't exhaust yourself."

"Mum come into the drawing room. I have something to tell you. And you Janet."

He was dreading her reaction. Although he was forgetting only he knew the truth. Elizabeth would be worried to hear Charles had gone missing, but she doesn't know Charles is dead.

"Mum, Dad's gone missing."

"What do you mean gone missing?"

"He didn't come home last night. The car is still here. I phoned the pub and he wasn't there last night. Then I phoned the police and they aren't worried yet. I don't know what else to do Mum."

His voice was becoming anxious. Suddenly he stopped pacing up and down. He looked at Elizabeth. He noticed she was so calm.

"Mum, aren't you worried?"

"This might come as a shock to you Robert and to you Janet, but I think your father has left me."

"Mum what makes you say that? I must say you don't seem bothered. You and Dad adored each other." Janet remarked.

"No Janet, I have known for a long time that your father was having an affair."

Robert sat down and rubbed his hands through his hair.

"But Mum, why didn't you leave him?" He said despairingly.

"I love my house, I love my lifestyle and most of all I love my children. Our bank accounts were joint so, I never had financial worries. Why should I have given it all up because of your father's stupidity?"

For a brief moment Robert felt a lack of respect for his mother. He quickly reminded himself he was in no state of mind to judge anyone, let alone his mother.

"How did you know?" Asked Janet.

"Because he was stupid and careless enough to leave a letter in a suit that he had asked me to take to the dry cleaners. It was a love letter and the bitch's name was Fiona."

Robert and Janet had never heard their mother use defamatory language before.

"Well, if he has left you Mum, why is your car still here?"

Robert was asking questions as if he didn't know the answers.

"Well she probably picked him up. As we share a car now, he has probably left it for me. It was the perfect opportunity, as we were all out of the house this weekend. I suppose it was just a matter of time. Robert, ring the police back and tell them you didn't know that he would be away for the weekend. Explain that I have just come home and told you. The villagers will find out soon enough, but I don't want rumours of your father going missing, that is just too preposterous for words."

19

Extreme Measures

Tommy Mullan was a gentleman. And a gentle man. He was quiet mannered and very softly spoken. Everyone knew Tommy and everyone loved Tommy. Yet despite being so loved, he didn't have anyone to love for himself.

He had reduced his hours in the local builders merchant and now worked afternoons from 2pm til 6pm. Customers with a little problem or concern, without a doubt, wanted to be served by Tommy. He was never short of words of wisdom and his customers with problems always left the shop feeling better than when they went in. Yes, he had words of wisdom for everyone, but none for himself.

All his life Tommy had struggled with the opposite sex. Shyness overshadowed him. Any woman who was fortunate enough to strike up a relationship with him would be treated like a queen. She in turn couldn't help but be seduced by his gentle loving nature. This could only happen once Tommy had jumped well and truly over his hurdle of shyness.

On Mondays, Wednesdays and Fridays at 11am Tommy would visit the church and light a candle to St. Anthony, to ask him to find a lovely lady for him. The only words of wisdom Tommy could give himself, was to ask St. Anthony. He had taken to asking about five months ago and was feeling a little ashamed of himself, as despair was creeping in. His feelings took him back to school, when religious instruction dictated not to despair, nor to presume: the sin of Despair and Presumption. Tommy being Tommy decided a visit to the confessional box was needed.

Even the black shade of the confessional box couldn't disguise Tommy from Father O'Keefe.

"Hello Tommy, how are you doing?"

"I'm well, thank you father."

"That's grand Tommy, now let me hear your confession."

The following Monday Tommy paid his visit to church at 11a.m. He lit his candle and apologised to St. Anthony for his despair. Suddenly he heard a sharp cry. Tommy rushed across to the statue of Our Lady, where a smart middle aged lady was obviously in some distress.

"What's happened my dear?"

"I lit a candle to Our Lady and tried to place it up on the back row. Look, all the front holders are full. I was careless and burnt my wrist on the lighted candles."

Tommy's shyness disappeared. His utmost thoughts were that someone needed help.

"Let me look at your wrist."

The woman turned her wrist over very gingerly.

"Ouch!"

"I think you need something on that. Let me take you to the Medical Centre across the road."

For a brief moment she forgot about her pain. She was thinking how kind and gentle Tommy was. It showed in his eyes.

"Thank you, that's so kind. And your name, what's your name?"

"I'm Tommy and you?"

"I'm Joan."

"Right Joan, give me your shopping and we'll get this wrist seen to."

The following Wednesday at 11a.m Tommy returned to see St. Anthony. He prayed in his mind.

Thank you St. Anthony for bringing Joan into my life, but if you don't mind me saying though, burning Joan's wrist could be seen as taking extreme measures. You'll be pleased to know, her wrist is fine now.

20

The Fancy Dress Party

Martha Brookes walked slowly down the hallway, her slippers hardly leaving the ground. The belt of her dressing gown trailed behind, mopping up drops of coffee that had spilled over from her excessively filled mug. She stooped down and, with her free hand, picked up the post. Martha was in her early 20s and still lived with her parents, so the majority of the post was always for them. Today, however, there was a card addressed to Martha. She dropped the rest of the post on the stairs and took the card to the privacy of her bedroom. Placing her coffee on the bedside table, she ripped open the envelope, letting it drop down onto the brightly coloured rug. Martha was surprised to see she had received an invitation to a fancy dress party. It couldn't have come at a more opportune moment. It was just a week ago when Martha received a cowardly text from her boyfriend Jason, to say he was ending their relationship. There was no doubt she was heartbroken, but Martha refused to accept bad treatment from anyone, let alone someone she loved and trusted. She didn't need to think twice, she instantly blocked him from her phone.

Martha was exhausted by her overwhelming depression. She had never experienced such emotional cruelty like Jason had put her through. Flopping down on her bed she silenced her sobs into her pillow, until the anaesthesia effects of sleep took over, allowing her broken heart and depression to temporarily take a rest,

The party was in three weeks time. Martha was undecided whether to go or not. Her mood was so low, she didn't want to take it to a party and infect everyone else.

Martha's first port of call when she needed some TLC and advice, was always her granny.

Martha's granny, also known as Joyce Bennett, was a strong independent woman. Life had moulded her that way. She had become a single parent to Martha's mother Yvonne, in her late teens. Despite her sometimes hard exterior, inwardly she remained as kind and gentle, as she was as a young girl.

Four hours later Martha was ringing her granny's doorbell. Number two, Lilac Close. She was so distraught she hadn't noticed that number four Lilac Close had now been sold, the house her granny had been fretting about for months. The weeds had taken control and swallowed up the lawn.

"Hello sweetheart. How lovely to see you. You always brighten my day."

Joyce opened her arms wide to hug her granddaughter. Granny's hugs meant the world to Martha and the love it gave off reduced her to tears.

"Oh my angel, what on earth is wrong?"

Martha opened up her heart completely. She told Joyce everything: her heartache, her depression and most of all, the person at the eye of the storm, Jason. Joyce reached for a tissue and gently wiped away Martha's tears.

"I thought he loved me Granny, but he didn't and I loved him so much."

"Well I am proud that you have given him the elbow. It shows you have self respect. I know you feel your world has fallen apart, but believe me, it won't last forever."

"Have you ever had your heart broken Granny?"

"Oh yes sweetheart. A long time ago now."

"What happened to you Granny?"

"Well it was different. Tom didn't break my heart, we both had broken hearts because of circumstances. We met at school when we were 15. Tom always knew that when he was 18 he and his family were moving to Canada. He really wanted to emigrate there and he wanted me to go with him, but it wasn't for me. Two months after he left I found out I was pregnant with your mum."

"Oh Granny that is so sad, but didn't you contact him?"

"No sweetheart I didn't. We had already decided that Canada was too far away to continue a relationship, so we agreed on a clean break and I didn't want to tread on his dreams. Besides, no mobile phones back then and I didn't have any contact details for him. That's how we wanted it. Letters, telephone calls and absence of the heart would have been too painful. I always believe, what will be, will be."

"Now then, back to you. There is only one place for anyone who lies and cheats on you and that is, out of your life. I promise you, one day you will look back at this time and wonder why you allowed him to break your little heart. However, that's in the future, but at this moment in time, we have to heal your broken heart. So, we have to think of something for you to look forward to."

"Thank you Granny. I am starting to feel a bit better now. Actually, I have been invited to a fancy dress party at my friend Tina's house. It's only a few streets away from you, so perhaps I could stay the night."

"Excellent. And I have just the thing you can wear. You are nice and slender, like I used to be, so I am sure it will fit you."

Martha managed a little smile.

"Gosh Granny what is it?"

"I will go and get it. Don't know why I kept it really. Anyway it's all packed away neatly in a suitcase."

Ten minutes later Joyce appeared holding garments wrapped in tissue paper. She carefully placed them on the table and peeled back the paper. Martha laughed out loud.

"Well, at least it has changed your tears to laughter, so that's a good sign."

"But Granny it's a school uniform."

"I know and it was mine. Look, my Head Girl badge is still pinned on the tie. You won't find a gymslip with big box pleats like this today."

Martha giggled. "Shall I try it on?"

"But of course, I'll put the kettle on."

Martha emerged 10 minutes later. Joyce was instantly transported back to her school girl days. It was like looking at herself. She felt a heavy sadness in her chest, wishing she could turn back time. Promptly turning her thoughts back to the now, she reminded herself it was Martha who needed her sadness lifted.

"What do you think Granny?"

"You look wonderful, just like a 60's innocent school girl, but I think I will take the Head Girl badge off for safe keeping. That was my pride and joy."

"I am so glad I came to see you. I feel so much better now."

"That's my girl. Let's have a hug".

It was the day of the party and Martha had kicked Jason firmly into touch. It felt quite strange for her to get dressed into clothes that her granny had worn all those years ago. To add finishing touches she put her hair in a 60's ponytail and didn't wear any makeup, apart from some white lipstick.

The party was within walking distance of her granny's house. Martha walked up the drive to the front door, which was elaborately decorated with every colour of balloon one could imagine. The door was open with a note stuck on the glass.

It read: *If you are in fancy dress, come in.*

Martha had noticed there was a car on the drive; it belonged to Tina's father. *I hope her parents won't be here,* she thought. She nervously pushed open the door. Robin Hood walked past her, while Snow White came down the stairs. Martha made her way to the kitchen, where she found

Tina reassuring her parents that the house would be looked after and the volume of the music would be acceptable to any potential complaining neighbour. There was another man there that Tina had never seen before. Tina's parents, Val and Roy, greeted Martha.

"Martha this is our old friend Tom, he is over from Canada. We are all going to a surprise birthday party."

"Hello Tom. Nice to meet you."

"Likewise Martha. Now where did you get that uniform? The girls in my school wore the very same."

"It was my granny's. It was her idea that I wear it. You must have gone to the same school then?"

"Yes. Redmond High. It was a long, long time ago."

Suddenly Martha's head was in a spin, her thoughts racing. *Tom, Canada, Redmond High School. Looks about the same age as Granny. What shall I do?*

She stuttered, "Are, are you over here for long, before returning to Canada?"

"Oh I'm not going back to Canada, I'm staying in blighty. In fact I have bought myself a little house. It's not far from here. Number four Lilac Close.

21

Mrs. Moran

The house was tall and solid as it stood in its Victorian splendour. The reliable steps that led up to the perfectly laid black and white minton tiled porch had, over the years, felt the weight of many a boot or shoe that had frequented the house, whether it be resident, or visitor.

There was one young boy, Bill Sutton, who had been captured by its splendour on his journey to school. He walked past it twice a day. He would stop and wish he could live in a house of such beauty. He loved every brick that built its walls, the tall chimneys and the most beautiful stained glass windows in the double front door. He loved the front door on winter mornings, as the light in the hallway was turned on, it displayed all the beauty of the glass in every detail.

On several occasions he saw the lady of the house looking out of the long window that overlooked the front garden. She would wave to Bill in a friendly manner. He eventually plucked up the courage to wave back. Bill did notice that she always seemed to wear pink.

Oh she is so lucky to live there., One day, he thought, *one day, I will live in a house like that. Or maybe even that house.*

After leaving school Bill went away to Edinburgh University where he attained a very respectable degree in architecture. He became successful in his profession and married his first love Mabel.

Mabel was a secretary in a firm of solicitors in the village where Bill had grown up. He wanted to live near his father, who was now a widower. Bill and Mabel bought a modest house on the outskirts of the village. He would often ask Mabel out for a walk to take her past the splendid Victorian house he had walked past so many times on his journeys to school and back. He would still stand and gaze in wonderment, pointing out little features in the brickwork and elegant chimneys, that Mabel hadn't even noticed.

Three years after they married, Mabel became pregnant and nine months later they were blessed with a little girl, who they named Alice. When Alice was five years old, her grandfather, Bill's father, sadly died. Bill was an only child and because of his busy work load, it took him almost two years to clear out and bring some saleability appeal to his father's house, which had now become his house.

Bill woke early one beautiful Saturday spring morning. Mabel always treated Bill to a delicious English 'fry up' on Saturdays.

"Mabel I think I will take a stroll before breakfast. I will enjoy my 'fry' so much better when I get back."

"Ok Bill. That will give me time to take a shower and have a relaxing cup of tea."

Of course there was only one way Bill was going to stroll and that was on that nostalgic journey he made to school. The trees lining the avenue, with their brand new fresh leaves made his heart skip a beat. He found them so intoxicating. He wanted to skip over the paving slabs, trying to avoid the cracks as he did as a child. He was nearing the house that he fell in love with many, many moons ago. *I wonder if the lady in pink will be looking out of the window. She's probably an old woman now.* An affectionate smile spread across his face.

On reaching the house he couldn't believe what he was seeing. What he saw almost looked alien. He saw hideous big red letters on a bright orange background. It stood dominant and yet proud. *Too proud* Bill thought. It looked cheap, tasteless and without class for such a beautiful specimen of architecture. Bill had an aesthetic eye and thought this tacky looking 'For Sale' board was completely unacceptable. He soon had a surge of excitement when a realisation descended upon him. He realised if he sold his house and his father's house, he could buy the house of his childhood dreams.

Twelve months later Bill Sutton and his lovely little family moved into 21, Manor Road, the house he had promised his inner child that he would live in one day.

Alice was so excited about her new home. She ran from room to room and up the winding staircase to choose a room for her bedroom. Mabel appeared at the foot of the stairs.

"Alice, the removal men are here. Have you chosen a room yet?"

"Yes Mummy, Elizabeth said I can have her room."

"What do you mean Elizabeth?"

"She's the lady I met on the stairs."

Mabel raised her eyebrows and let out a loud sigh.

"Bill we are not going to get her to sleep tonight. She now has an imaginary friend."

"Oh she'll settle down soon, she's just excited with the move," Bill laughed.

Alice continued to talk to Elizabeth and include her in her life. Bill and Mabel had made a joint decision not to make an issue over Elizabeth. They thought the less said would make Elizabeth disappear.

Alice loved to help Mabel with the housework. Her favourite job was to wax polish the old desk at the top of the stairs on the landing. It had been in her father's house when he was a child, and his father's before. She loved how the polish could be smelt all over the house and she could also talk to Elizabeth at the same time, but she had learnt to keep their conversations to herself.

As the years had gone by, Alice had got to know every scratch and mark, new and old, on the beautiful desk that stood at the top of the stairs. She polished it religiously every Friday morning. Alice didn't work on Fridays. She was a self employed holistic therapist and was fortunate enough to be able to use a spare bedroom as her treatment room. She found it had a lovely energy and she knew Elizabeth was often there. She also knew that no matter how much she loved living in her childhood home, it was now time to find a home of her own and flee the nest. Finding the money for a deposit, however, was a big stumbling block.

"Alice when you go into the village to pick up your dad's prescription, would you get a newspaper for him. It's the Grand National tomorrow and you know how he likes a little flutter."

"Ok Mum, but I am just going to polish the desk before I go."

"You and that desk. I'm sure you must have been a maid in a previous life."

Alice went into the scullery to get the polish and dusters. She walked slowly up the stairs, remembering how excited she had felt all those years ago on the day they moved in. It was also her first encounter with Elizabeth as she floated downstairs in her beautiful pink gown.

Opening the tin of polish she patted her duster into the soft lavender wax. Carefully and lovingly she circled the duster over the desk, the smell of lavender filling the air. She sensed Elizabeth was there. Alice thought she should tell Elizabeth of her plans to move, but reassured her it might be in a few years as she had to save for a deposit.

"Do you understand what I mean about a deposit Elizabeth? I imagine you had a very grand life, without any concerns over money."

A cold breeze brushed down the right side of Alice's body and seemed to reach her large yellow duster that was perched on the banister, waiting to bring a lustrous shine to the desk. The breeze blew it over the edge and it fell into the hallway below. Alice was somewhat startled. She was hoping that she hadn't upset Elizabeth by telling her what her plans were. Running downstairs she retrieved her duster. She looked up and saw Elizabeth walk away from the desk.

"I didn't mean to upset you Elizabeth," Alice said in a panting breath as she ran up the stairs.

Elizabeth had gone.

With everything on her mind Alice was using more elbow grease than usual. The shine was starting to appear. She went over and over the same place several times. A new mark had appeared. She rubbed and rubbed without success, it just wouldn't shift. Taking a closer look Alice could see it was a scratch. *How did that happen?* She thought. The more she polished she could see it wasn't a scratch at all, it was writing. It read, *Mrs. Moran.* Puzzling as it was, she reasoned it with herself by thinking her mother or father must have written something at the desk and it had gone through the paper. She was quite surprised and very annoyed at their carelessness.

Alice washed her hands, grabbed her coat and scarf from the hallstand and walked into the village. The bell on the chemist door rang out as Alice went in to get her dad's prescription. She was surprised to see a new assistant behind the counter. She was a small, trim lady of advancing years with soft grey hair.

"Hello. You're new aren't you?" Alice inquired.

"Yes my dear. I'm Maggie. I retired eighteen months ago from the hospital pharmacy, but I did miss something to do. So when this came up for two days a week I jumped at the chance."

"Oh that's wonderful," Alice remarked. "I have seen you before though."

"Well I have lived here all my life; I was born in the village. Anyway how can I help you?"

"Oh yes, I was forgetting," Alice laughed. "I would like the prescription for my dad, Bill Sutton."

"Certainly. What address is it?"

"21 Manor Road."

"Oh you live in the haunted house."

Alice was taken aback and she didn't want to give anything away.

"Do I? Tell me more."

"Well it happened many years ago, even before my time. It is said the lady of the house, Elizabeth Moran, was a very keen horse rider. She was out riding one day. Her horse bolted, threw her off and she died instantly. It was only very close friends and family of course, that called her Elizabeth. She was always known as Mrs. Moran. Apparently her horse was called Pink Lady. People who have seen her call her the lady in pink, as she wears a pink gown. I bet you didn't imagine you would have a history lesson about your house when you came in to pick up your dad's prescription."

Alice gave a false laugh. "I certainly didn't. I must look out for her. Did you say her name was Elizabeth?"

"Yes, Elizabeth. Mrs. Elizabeth Moran." Maggie said in a ghostly manner.

"Thank you Maggie, nice to meet you. I hope I sleep tonight. Bye."

The two women laughed in unison.

As Alice was making her way to the paper shop her thoughts were taken up with her conversation with Maggie. She always knew she had a sixth sense and connected with spirit, but she was now dissatisfied with her own explanation of how the letters *Mrs. Moran* were engraved in the wood on the desk.

After buying her newspaper, Alice was feeling a little exhausted after her morning drama over the letters on the desk and the very sad story of how Elizabeth died, which upset Alice to say the least. Needing to recharge her batteries she made her way to the village cafe, The Coffee Pot, for an injection of caffeine and ten minutes rest and recuperation. Upon arriving Alice decided a cup of camomile tea and a large oaty cookie would be far more beneficial and soothing to the senses.

She placed her shopping bag on the chair beside her. The newspaper jutted out from the top of her bag. There was a little square box to the top left of the front page and inside the box it read, *Pick a Winner for Tomorrow's Grand National. If only* she thought.

Alice pulled the newspaper out and opened it to the page that listed the riders. *Oh my word,* she thought. *There are so many, I wouldn't have a clue. Dad always said pick what you fancy.'* She scanned down the list, thinking she didn't fancy any of them. Suddenly near to the bottom of the list, her eyes stopped to a definite halt. They stayed there for quite some time with a fixed stare. She really couldn't believe what she was reading. The horse she fancied was called Mrs. Moran. In an instant, everything became clear. *It was Elizabeth who wrote her name in the desk. She purposely blew the duster over the banister, knowing that I would have to go and fetch it. That's when she wrote her name. I saw her walking away from the desk, just after I picked up the duster.* Alice's thoughts were working over time. *What was she trying to tell me? I told her I need a deposit for a house. She must be telling me to put money on this horse as a way of getting my deposit.* Alice couldn't imagine her thoughts could get any more hyper. She took a slow walk home and thought she would ask her dad what he thought about Mrs. Moran.

As Alice approached her house, she saw Elizabeth at the window on the landing, which overlooked the front garden. She was looking down at Alice smiling and waving. Alice went in through the kitchen door. Her mum and dad were sitting at the kitchen table enjoying a cup of tea. They all exchanged greetings, then Alice handed her dad his prescription along with the newspaper.

"See if you can pick a winner Dad."

"I'll have a good try. Why don't you have a go?"

"Funny you should say that Dad, I have had a look and there is a horse that I fancy – Mrs. Moran."

Bill scanned the list. "I can't seem to find it."

"It's near the bottom Dad."

"Oh crikey. You'd be lucky if it won. It's a hundred to one."

"What does that mean?"

"It means Alice, that it's not very well fancied."

Alice gave a little chuckle, "Oh I don't think I'll bother then." Crossing her fingers behind her back, like she did as a child, when she was lying.

"Well I am just going to meditate for half an hour. See you later."

Mabel looked across the table at Bill.

"Where did we get her from Bill? Meditation, essential oils, yoga and she still talks to her imaginary friend. I often hear her."

"Yes Mabel, but she's a kind soul, what more could we ask for?"

Alice had settled on her meditation stool and chosen one of her favourite CDs with beautiful calming sounds of singing bowls, birdsong and soothing wind chimes. After some deep breathing in preparation for her meditation, Alice connected with Elizabeth and asked her to show her presence if she thought it wise for her to place a bet on Mrs. Moran. She was twenty minutes into her meditation. Elizabeth hadn't shown her presence, when suddenly Alice felt a slight heaviness on her shoulder, a cold breeze whipped around her body. She knew Elizabeth was there. Alice opened her eyes and saw Elizabeth fading into the wall. Elizabeth turned and lifted her dainty hand giving a delicate yet caring wave. Alice smiled back at her and whispered "Thank you."

She was now convinced she would put a considerable amount of her savings on Mrs. Moran to win the Grand National. Alice had a deep belief in the universe and how it provided in many mysterious ways.

Next morning there was an icy chill in the air. The sun was breaking through the fine misty morning, attempting to thaw that icy chill. Alice had made a plan. After her daily Qigong practice, followed by a light breakfast, she would drive to a nearby town, which was thirty minutes away. She didn't know anyone there, so it was unlikely she would meet anyone she knew and she certainly wouldn't know anyone who worked at the bookmakers. She had told her parents that she was off to visit a friend for the day. Her little car was waiting faithfully for her on the drive. It was covered in the dampness of the day. The layer of thin ice on the windscreen had almost thawed. Quickly and efficiently Alice run her telescopic scraper over the windscreen. As she did so, she could sense Elizabeth was somewhere around. Glancing up to the landing window she saw Elizabeth once again, looking down waving and smiling, as if to reassure Alice that all would be well. Alice waved back, got in her car and made her journey to place her bet on Mrs. Moran.

Alice walked into the bookmakers, she felt confident and had no qualms about placing her bet. She walked to the counter.

"Can you help me please? I have never placed a bet before, but I would like to place a bet on Mrs. Moran in the Grand National."

"No problem. I'll fill out the betting slip for you. I presume you want it each way?"

"Each way? What does that mean?"

"It means you will win something if your horse comes in first, second, third or fourth."

"Oh no. I just want to bet on it coming first."

"Are you sure, it is a hundred to one?"

"Yes, I'm sure."

Jack the Bookie gave a wry smile.

"How much would you like to bet?"

"£500 please," Alice said confidently as she placed her money on the high counter.

"Are you absolutely sure? You do realise if it loses, you lose all your money" Jack stressed.

"Oh, I'm absolutely sure"

We have a right one here. She must have more money than sense. Jack thought.

"Ok, if you say so. There's your betting slip. Keep that safe. You'll need it if it wins," he said trying to keep a straight face. "Without it you won't be able to claim your winnings. Have a good day."

"You too. Thank you so much for your help."

"My pleasure."

Alice arrived home at 6pm. Elizabeth wasn't waiting at the landing window like she usually did. Her parents went out for dinner on Saturday nights, so she had the house to herself. Enthusiastically Alice unlocked the front door.

"Elizabeth, Elizabeth", she called out. "I did it. I placed my bet on Mrs. Moran. The man at the bookmakers was so helpful."

Suddenly Alice sensed a silence she hadn't felt before. Running upstairs she couldn't feel Elizabeth's presence. She had never felt the house so empty.

"Elizabeth, where are you?" Alice called out.

Returning downstairs Alice went into the lounge to catch the news. At the precise moment she turned on the television, the re-run of the Grand National was being played. She could hardly watch. The commentator's voice was hoarse with excitement.

"I have never seen anything like it."

Alice's head was in a whirl, she couldn't take it all in. The commentator continued.

"This little beauty is coming up on the inside, she's going to do it, she's running her little heart out."

"Who's running her little heart out?" Alice screamed.

"She's done it, against all the odds, she's done it. Mrs. Moran the hundred to one outsider has only gone and won the Grand National.

"Yeah!" Alice cheered, clapping her hands.

The news went to the present time.

"We have some breaking news. Mrs, Moran who won today's Grand National very sadly collapsed and died an hour after she won her race."

Alice was devastated. Her happiness created by her win, that is enabling her to put a deposit on a house and more, was now completely over shadowed by the death of Mrs. Moran. She walked slowly upstairs to look at the letters *Mrs. Moran* carved in the desk. And like Elizabeth they had gone. Elizabeth was finally at rest.

22

Memories

I drive past my childhood home. I see the memories inside. I see them with my mind and not with my eyes. I see my mother cleaning windows, with her shammy leather tight in hand. I see the breadman calling round. I can see his wicker basket, filled with bread of white and brown. I can see his leather money bag all shiny with wear.

Where have these moments gone? They can't have disappeared. Their energies are somewhere, maybe stored within the walls.

I can see myself skipping along the pavement, avoiding the cracks. You couldn't tread on a crack, otherwise, something awful would happen, but apart from the cracks, there were no worries, just freedom, like a bird in the sky. Those precious memories of golden days.

School friends' faces outside the school gate. I can see them clearly. Precious friends of yesterday. I want to reach out to touch them and be where we once were. Can I turn back a chapter as I do with a book, but not a chapter of words, a chapter of time, just to have another look. The energies of our memories will never fade away.

They are all there somewhere, neatly filed away in the archives of our mind.